FINDING LOVE IN ALASKA

Under the

MOOSELTOE

Copy Editor: Write Girl Editing Services

Cover Design: Alt 19 Creative

Proofreading: FictionEdit.com

Chapter One

Ava

"Ed, step away from the Christmas wreath. Those aren't even *real* berries." Ava Monroe didn't have time to be detained by a decoration-eating moose. Especially not Sunset Ridge's local celebrity.

She bit her lip and glanced at her watch. Anyone who'd lived in the Alaskan tourist town for any length of time had at least one Ed story to tell. The moose had a definite habit of getting in the way when it was the least convenient.

His timing was part of his charm.

The bull moose didn't seem impressed by Ava's demands and continued sniffing the wreath hanging off her duplex neighbor's railing. She would leave the animal to his criminal mischief, if only her car wasn't parked on the other side of him.

"Please move?" she asked nicely.

Ed didn't budge.

With a groan, she shoved a hand into her over-stuffed purse and wiggled her fingers through the contents. It was almost like one of the Halloween blind boxes Mrs. Baker used to make for her third-grade class, except without the peeled grapes filling in for eyeballs.

Ava froze, fingers now curled around a buzzing phone instead of the car keys she needed. *Wait. Could I make Christmas-themed blind boxes that parents might be interested in buying?* She'd have to think about it. Time might be against her.

Excited with her new idea, Ava pulled her still-buzzing phone out of her purse and glanced at the caller ID. *Mom? Again!* "Just great," she mumbled, energy deflating. Ava sent her mother to voicemail for the second time that morning.

Ed, now pawing at the air as if he could knock the wreath down, shifted his wide hips a little farther in Ava's direction. Dropping her useless phone back into the abyss, she glanced at Brayden's bay window. Elsie, her neighbor's golden retriever, watched the scene eagerly, pacing along the slightly jutted window.

Elsie's anxious presence wasn't doing anything to deter Ed. The moose hardly seemed affected by the whining dog.

"Come on, Brayden," she muttered under her breath. "Maybe investigate why your dog is going nuts." Even though she'd been avoiding him these past couple of weeks, she longed to see the blue of his eyes right about now. Maybe Ed would move *then*.

Or maybe Brayden wasn't even here and she was on her own.

Scanning the area for a secondary escape route, Ava spotted Brayden's open garage door. His truck filled most of the narrow space, but there was no sign of him. Okay. So he *was* here and just didn't care if Elsie threw a fit.

Ed yanked a plastic berry from the wreath and spit it on the ground. Ava wanted to cheer. *Yes! Yucky plastic. Now go away*. But Ed, if nothing else, was a tenacious moose. One bite of plastic was never going to be enough. Ed widened his stance, settling in for the full demolition.

"I don't have time for this," Ava said to Ed, her words a plea. Her ridiculously long to-do list raced through her mind as she fumbled for her keys with

3

thickly gloved hands. *Pick up the ribbon order. Get sugar cookie lattes for Glenda and Becca. Review the schedule.*

Her only hope was to skirt around Ed. *Interview Rilee. Check the website for online orders.* "Just need to make a run for it," she told herself even as the list continued in the back of her mind. *Assemble as many baskets as possible.*

Ava glanced down at her short boots, contemplating how they'd stand up against the deep snow surrounding the plowed drive. Most days she loved this duplex for its privacy in the middle of town. Right now, however, the lack of close neighbors was downright annoying. "Thank goodness for auto start," she mumbled, her breath frosting in the chilly air.

Her buzzing phone drew her attention to the purse again. "Mom, I swear . . ." Ava wanted to ignore it, but there was always a chance it was the store. Or her brother. Or her best friend, Kinley.

Nope, Mom again.

Freeing her fingertips from her mittens, she snapped a photo of Ed, since he didn't seem in a hurry, and sent it to Mom with one word. *Detained.* If Ed had to make her late for everything else today, at least she could use the situation to her advantage.

Mom had been blowing up Ava's phone for weeks now.

It was partially Ava's fault. She'd been avoiding most of the calls, sending her mom straight to voicemail. But Mom had a way of drawing the truth out of her, and this was one time Ava couldn't admit what was *really* wrong.

The family store, one passed down to generation after generation of women in her family, was nearing foreclosure. A business that shouldn't even *have* a mortgage. She had ten days to come up with the delinquent balance or the bank was taking it. On Christmas Eve, no less.

"But I've got a plan," Ava promised the phone in her hand. A huge, all-in gamble that had as great a chance of failing as it had of succeeding. Christmas gift baskets. The sudden idea caused Ava to max out her credit cards, empty her savings, and take her biggest risk yet. And she hadn't shared it with Mom. Ava planned to brag about it *after* she sold a few dozen baskets.

With any luck, Mom would never know how close the Forget Me Not Boutique had come to closing its doors.

Mom: Call me later. Geraldine Franks' grandson moved home. You should go out with him!

"Ugh!" If Mom's inability to let the store go wasn't overbearing enough, in pursuit of more grandkids, she was also on a mission to find Ava a husband. Ava entertained the urge to text back that her sister Jamie already had the Monroe siblings covered when it came to grandkids. It was the reason her parents retired to Minnesota three years ago.

Before she could free her mitten-clad fingers a second time, Elsie let out a chorus of excited barks from the living room window. Ed had the wreath on the ground and was yanking off plastic berries. Ava cringed, watching Ed destroy the wreath Brayden recently purchased at her store.

"Ed, leave that alone!" A plastic berry sailed her way, bouncing off her leg.

Elsie continued to bark from the window, which only seemed to aggravate the beast. Goofy grin or not, the lovable local favorite was still capable of trampling Ava flat. With the snow flurries now falling in heavy sheets, it might be spring before anyone found her.

"Look, I really have to go." Hoping to escape, Ava took one cautious step toward the edge of the driveway, but Ed wasn't having any of it. He began to trot *at* her. "Crap!" She shuffled backward, praying she could make it to her front door—or any door. She didn't have time to get run over by a moose today.

With each step, Ed picked up speed.

Desperate, Ava darted into Brayden's garage. It was only by some miracle he hadn't realized it was open while she was outside facing the beast. She zipped for the door, palmed the garage door opener, and fell into his kitchen.

Brayden Young held a coffee mug inches from his lips, as if he were about to take a sip. It lingered midair as his gaze fell on her, one eyebrow raising. "Ava?" He set his mug on the counter beside a laptop. The forget-me-not blue on the screen drew her gaze. He pushed off the counter, one hand closing his laptop and the other reclaiming his mug. "Everything okay?"

It was entirely possible—and probable—that Brayden already knew her deepest, darkest secret. She'd steered clear of him ever since he gave her the final notice letter he claimed to have opened on accident. But now, she couldn't run.

"Ed," she finally said, pointing to the living room window where Elsie still paced and whined. She wondered what had him so engrossed on his laptop that he remained oblivious to the commotion outside. "Did you really *not* notice?" Ava asked, still panting to catch her breath.

"Elsie makes the same fuss over squirrels and questionable tree branches," Brayden said, flashing her a smirk on his way to the window. *That* smirk, one capable of melting an unsuspecting woman into a puddle of goo, was one of his most dangerous weapons. But Ava was ready for it. Besides, he had his chance months ago and blew it.

Didn't matter anyway. Ever since the day of Kinley's engagement party, she'd kept her distance. The guilty look on his face when he shoved a ripped envelope with a foreclosure notice through her car window, promising he hadn't read it, made her extra cautious of him.

Ava didn't need *anyone*, let alone her neighbor, knowing how dire things were for her store.

"Is he gone?" she asked, referring to Ed. Anything to put space between them. Once she saved the Forget Me Not Boutique, they could be friends again. Until then, she'd stick with slipping Elsie treats on their adjoined deck and avoiding Brayden at all costs.

"Nope. Ed's right outside the garage." He shook

his head, scratching an eager Elsie behind the ears. His gentle fingers seemed to calm the pup. "This town has it all, doesn't it?"

"Part of its charm." Ava's gaze swept over Brayden, jealous of his plaid patterned pajama bottoms. She couldn't remember the last time she had a day off, much less the freedom to be in pajamas this late in the morning. Though Brayden was still a big mystery to most of Sunset Ridge, she doubted he had a to-do list that grew longer every second he wasn't working to whittle it down.

No, Brayden worked from his home-based woodworking shed, crafting bookshelves and rocking chairs to order. He could work when it suited him.

With a deep breath, Ava dared to join him at the bay window to assess the situation. The moose was back at the wreath, shredding the poor thing in retribution for its lack of edible bits. Ed was known for his stubbornness, but this was ridiculous. "Not really a chance I can get to my car, is there?"

"I wouldn't risk it." Brayden sipped his coffee, not the least unsettled that Ed was tearing apart his wreath. If she wasn't mistaken, he was fascinated by the beast. "Guess I'll need another one," he said about the decoration that was now little more than a pile of pine branches scattered on the ground. "Want some coffee while you wait it out?"

"He'll move."

Brayden stretched his neck to get another look. "I know I'm not from Alaska, but I wouldn't bet on it. He looks pretty determined." He returned to the small kitchen that was a mirror of her own and fixed her a mug. "Why don't you park in the garage anymore?"

"It's full."

"Of what?"

Ava scanned the open living area, surprised to find Christmas decorations scattered throughout—a string of garland along the fireplace mantle, a metal snowman hanging from the wall, and a holiday throw pillow adorned with northern lights on the couch. All things she sold in her store. Maybe he still felt guilty about standing her up for their date. But that was ridiculous. Months had passed.

Yet the more she looked around, the more holiday items she recognized from the Forget Me Not. The only thing missing was a tree, which she didn't carry. It made her feel ashamed that her own place didn't have a single decoration yet. She'd been too busy.

"Ava?"

"Supplies," she finally answered. "The garage is full of supplies." Every spare inch of her garage was lined with rickety shelves she'd picked up cheap at a store closing in Anchorage. Those shelves were filled with baskets, garland, and a wide assortment of Alaskan-made gifts. Her garage held either her salvation or the final nail in her coffin.

"I know it's not a spacious garage, but your car isn't *that* big."

Ava studied the mug he slid to her, not eager to meet his assessing eyes on the opposite side of the breakfast bar. She felt too vulnerable. Brayden knew too much, even if he never admitted to it. Before she could find words to swiftly change the subject, her phone buzzed *again*.

She set the mug down so she could scour her purse for the offending electronic device. *Mom, again.* "She just doesn't give up," Ava mumbled. She jabbed at the ignore button with gusto, sending the call to voicemail. *Again.* The picture of Ed really should've bought her more than three minutes of silence.

"I thought I was the only one with an overbearing mother," Brayden said with a chuckle, hiding most of his smile behind his cup. A Christmas mug, handcrafted in Kenai. Another item the Forget Me Not housed on its shelves.

"She's called *three* times just this morning," Ava explained before finally taking a sip of coffee, savoring the hint of peppermint.

"Mine's called four."

Ava nearly choked on her second sip. "You're making that up."

Brayden pushed a couple of buttons then slid his phone across the counter. The call log displayed on the screen.

Ava pulled it a little closer, counting with a quick finger scroll. "*Ten* times yesterday?"

"That doesn't include the text messages."

The tension between them eased the slightest. "Didn't realize we had that in common. Is your mom also trying to subtly control your life from thousands of miles away?"

"Thousands of miles," Brayden agreed. "But she's not subtle at all."

"Oh, yeah? What is your mom trying to decide for you?"

"You know, the usual. What I do for a living, where I live, who I marry."

Ava raised an eyebrow at that. "*Who* you marry?"

"Oh, yeah." Almost on cue, Brayden's phone lit up, buzzing across the counter. "Five. I'm winning."

Ava realized that despite months of being neighbors, she still didn't know much about him. He had perfected vague answers. She knew he was from Texas, but not *why* he moved to Alaska. He spoke of his mom, sister, and grandma, but never anything personal. She didn't even know their names. Brayden was a mystery to most of Sunset Ridge and seemed to prefer it that way. "Who does she want you to marry?"

"Today?"

"Wow, that bad?"

"She's a determined woman. Luckily, I'm extra stubborn." Brayden turned to refill his coffee. "Why are *you* avoiding your mom?"

With Elsie still firmly planted at the window mildly whining, Ava gave up the idea of leaving soon. She settled on a barstool. "She retired from the family store almost four years ago, but you wouldn't know it by how involved she still wants to be. She stalks my website, tells me I'm pricing everything wrong, and doesn't approve of most of the changes I've made." Ava's phone lit with another string of texts about a date with some guy named Pete. She dropped it back in her purse, hoping it'd get lost until

New Year's. "If that's not enough, she constantly badgers me about grandkids and sets me up on dates."

Brayden's eyebrow rose at that.

"My parents moved to Minnesota to be near the only sibling who's married with a kid—my *baby* sister, Jamie. But she's constantly on Chase and me to create more. Never mind that Jamie's nearly ready to pop with baby number two."

"Chase, your brother?"

"Yeah." Ava sipped her coffee, but it was now cold. "But since Chase was actually married once before, she's on me a lot more." She sucked in a deep breath, willing the memories of her former best friend Laurel, eloping with her brother behind her back and disappearing six months later, to go away. She had enough on her mind without old wounds festering too. "I wish I could get her to back off. It's embarrassing having your mom set you up in your hometown, you know? This place isn't *that* big. So if I say no, then I'm the bad guy. Even when they stand *me* up." She cleared her throat, but didn't apologize for the jab that Brayden also deserved. "I'm half tempted to invent a fake boyfriend just to make it stop."

Ava moved to the coffee pot to freshen her cup,

an ominous feeling washing over her as Brayden remained silent behind her.

"That's not a half-bad idea."

"What?"

"Making up a significant other for some reprieve."

Ava took a cautious sip. "I wish it'd work, but my mom would want proof." She let out a laugh. "Knowing her, she'd demand photographic evidence and probably badger my brother and friends for details about how serious it really is."

"Pictures . . ." Brayden drew out the word as if pondering something deeply. "Maybe it could work for me, too." He spun toward her. "What if you and I pretended to—"

"What?" Ava shook her head, suddenly suffocated by their close proximity. She scurried out of the kitchen and back to her barstool. "No, that's not what I meant."

"It's just pictures," Brayden continued. "We dress up in Christmas sweaters, take a few selfies, and send them to our mothers. At the very least, it should stop the ten-plus phone calls a day for a while. Maybe let us enjoy the holidays in peace."

"No."

"You dislike me that much?" Brayden asked, as if

hurt.

"What? I don't dislike you."

"You've been avoiding me for two weeks. If it weren't for Ed, you'd *still* be avoiding me. Why?"

Because Ava was *not* about to answer that question, she gave in to the lesser evil. "Fine. Pictures. But be warned, it won't end there. You'll be dragged into a Christmas sweater Skype event too."

"Sounds fun."

Ava laughed. "You really have no idea what you're getting yourself into, do you?"

"Desperate times. And both our moms will be thousands of miles away. How hard could it be to pull it off? At least until Christmas is over. Then we can tell them it was all a joke if you want. Get a rise out of *them* for a change."

"Pictures," Ava muttered, wondering how she could convince her mom the relationship was real if she didn't post about it on her social media. "Why did I ever teach my mom how to use Facebook?"

"What's that?"

"Nothing." She could head off Chase, beg him to play along for the sake of her sanity. Bribe him with the Bonita's Christmas cranberry scones if necessary. And Kinley. Surely she'd play along for Ava's sake. A few pictures and one Christmas sweater virtual event. Simple enough. Ava slipped off her hat and fluffed out her hair. "Okay, I'm ready."

Brayden laughed again.

"What?"

"You don't know my mother. It has to be convincing."

"Is there something wrong with what I'm wearing?"

"No." He said the word so quickly, she knew he meant it. "It's just my mom, she's not easily fooled. Couples do things together. We need to look more like a couple. And I'm in my pajamas, in case you didn't notice."

Ava approached the living room window because she *had* noticed. An enormous relief swept through her when she spotted Ed finally headed toward the trees, even if he was taking his sweet time leaving. This fake relationship, no matter how simple, was a bad idea. But her buzzing purse cemented her decision. "Fine. I'll be home this afternoon."

"I'll be here."

Dashing for the front door, Ava asked, "Think you can get out of your jammies by then?"

"I might even shower." He held his Christmas mug in toast. "See you later, fake girlfriend."

Chapter Two

BRAYDEN

Brayden kept an eye on Ed as Ava drove away, mercifully without incident.

"What a sly ol' moose, huh, Elsie?" He scratched the golden's ears as she leaned against his legs. He hated every minute of awkwardness that emerged after giving Ava that darn letter. Their fractured friendship had been nearly repaired until that mailbox mix-up. Every day she avoided him since he almost flung the foreclosure notice at her riddled him with guilt.

Yes, he read it.

But not on purpose.

He doubted Ava would accept it had been an accident. A result of letting his own mail stack up so high in his mailbox that he went through the envelopes on autopilot. He never would've opened her letter if he noticed it wasn't addressed to him.

He told her he hadn't read it, if only to save her embarrassment. But he knew her store—the Forget Me Not Boutique—was days from foreclosure. Ten, to be precise. Ava wasn't one to accept help without a fight, either. Her pride often stood in the way for simple things, like offering to carry in groceries or shovel her steps. She had no idea he could write a check for the delinquent balance and hardly notice a dent in his bank account. Even if he offered, she'd scoff at him.

Instead, he'd placed dozens of online orders in his grandma's name, shipping them to Austin for her to share with the other condo dwellers in her retirement community. Just last week she warned him that if he sent one more batch of moose ornaments, her neighbors might revolt. He compromised by sending a round of forget-me-not wreaths.

Brayden returned to his empty coffee cup, making a mental note that he hadn't shipped Grandma any of *those* yet. He glanced about his living room, sparsely decorated except for the holiday decor Ava stocked. He'd seen her look around, noticing her things in his home. Thank goodness, she hadn't seen his spare room where twice as much was piled in boxes.

He reached in the cookie jar—a moose sitting on a log—and pulled out one of the homemade dog treats Ava also sold. "Sit," he said, holding it up for Elsie to see. She promptly dropped her butt to the floor, tail swishing softly on the hardwood. He tossed it to her, following it with another shortly after. He'd stockpiled so many dog treats that he had to freeze some.

But it still wasn't enough to save her store. He yearned to do more.

Most wouldn't understand why helping Ava save her business mattered so much to him. But he felt certain Grandpa would've done the same in his position. Brayden released a sigh so heavy Elsie looked up at him. "Wish you could've met him, girl. He would've liked you."

Elsie's tail wagged leisurely as she followed him to his bedroom. She curled up on the edge of his bed as he showered and got dressed.

Helping Ava's store had also been a welcome distraction from a future he wasn't ready to dwell on. One that *should* eventually mean saying goodbye to his quiet, comfortable life in Sunset Ridge and taking over a corporation once his mother retired. He promised as much when he left, but the desire to abandon his new life was nonexistent. He liked it here.

Part of him never wanted to leave.

No one in this cozy Alaska town knew who he really was, or that his net worth included eight figures. Though he did keep to himself more than most, the townsfolk were friendly and accepted him as one of their own. The locals loved his handcrafted bookshelves, desks, and nightstands, and it allowed him to hone skills his late grandpa had taught him.

Coming from a fast-paced lifestyle, Sunset Ridge granted him a rare opportunity to slow down and realize what he'd been taking for granted while working every waking hour. That's why he loved it here. No heavy expectations weighed on his shoulders. No intense deadlines hovered over him. No pressure to prepare to take over the family business existed.

Never mind that Mom wasn't planning to retire for two more years. She expected him not only to visit for this holiday, but to show up with a moving truck. She was tired of his absence and what she considered to be a frivolous waste of time. She'd allowed him to mourn and reevaluate his life, and she was having no more of it. This fake relationship might buy him a little more time before the inevitable decision. Or it might completely backfire.

But Brayden wasn't ready to return to Texas.

He might not ever be ready.

For years, he operated on autopilot, working around the clock to help grow the family marketing firm into the multi-million-dollar national success it had become. Even after his grandpa passed, he threw himself into his work to ward off the grief. Grandma's pleading for him to take time off and take a step back went ignored.

Until a near-death experience changed everything.

He shouldn't even be alive, but he was. That final sign too obvious to ignore, he finally heeded Grandma's advice. Once cleared from the hospital, he packed his truck and headed north to the small town his grandparents honeymooned at decades ago. Mom thought he was off his rocker driving all the way to Alaska by himself in winter. He went anyway.

He'd hoped the trip up the Alcan Highway would help him figure everything out. But the scenic days-long drive left him with more questions than answers.

Seven days after leaving Texas, Brayden arrived at the Sunset Ridge Lodge and prayed they had an open room. The Whitmore sisters loved the honeymoon story topped off with the postcard with worn edges Grandma gave him for the trip.

Brayden expected to stay a few days. Maybe a couple of weeks.

The longer he decided not to check out, the less he wanted to leave at all.

"C'mon, Elsie. We have a coffee table to work on." The golden's tail wagged, her nose pointed at the treat canister next to the coffee maker. "Okay, *one*. You've already had three today. Four if you snuck over to Ava's earlier, which we both know you did."

Elsie tilted her head, doe eyes staring at him in innocence. He tossed her a treat then filled a travel mug with the leftover coffee.

During his second week in Sunset Ridge, Brayden happened across an opportunity to purchase a rental property. Then another. Weeks turned into months as he quietly bought up the houses under an LLC. He didn't need the passive income, but it felt good to know he could make ends meet without a dime of his family's money.

The added bonus was that he was giving neglected homes a second chance. His grandpa had always been a big advocate of giving back in big but quiet ways to small communities. Not even Ava knew Brayden was her landlord, and he liked it that way. Only his realtor and property manager knew he was the CEO of Northern Lights Properties.

After slipping on his coat, he opened the sliding-glass door and Elsie trotted out onto the deck. The freshly fallen snow covered only some of her early morning paw prints that led to Ava's back door. His next door neighbor definitely had a soft spot for his dog. "She's not home," he told the dog when she stared down the joined deck in contemplation. "C'mon. We have work to do."

When he came across this duplex with the wood-working shed in its backyard several months ago, he not only bought the property but moved into one side the day he closed on the duplex. The private acreage surrounded by trees with its central location was perfect. It allowed Brayden to stay hidden as often as he liked, right smack dab in the middle of town.

He adopted Elsie from a shelter the day after he

settled in and lost himself to one woodworking project after another until that too became a business. Working with his hands instead of through conference calls and emails made him feel closer to the grandpa he'd lost. Had Ava Monroe not signed the lease to move into the other side of the duplex, he might never have come up for air.

He liked it here.

He had a life here. Friends. Purpose. One he wasn't eager to abandon. But lately, Mom had been less than patient with his choices. She wanted him back home where he belonged. Home and married. His mother's idea of a notice of intent that he wouldn't decide to make Alaska his permanent residence. He knew she wouldn't officially announce her retirement until he was settled in Texas.

Inside the shed, he lit the woodstove as Elsie settled into her bed. But before he could gather his tools, his phone buzzed. A string of text messages about his responsibilities to his family filled his screen. Mom on one of her tirades again. "I'm not coming home," he mumbled to the phone, resisting the urge to text back.

More than anything, he loved the freedom to work on his projects at any hour. Sometimes, he worked all through the night and slept half the day away. It was glorious not to be controlled by a strict schedule. To get lost in a process done by hand rather than chasing down the next high-dollar portfolio. He didn't have to pitch his products because they sold themselves. And if they didn't sell, it didn't matter.

Settling into a rolling stool with sandpaper in hand, he got to work on the coffee table a local teacher requested as a gift for her sister.

He liked this slower pace. He liked Sunset Ridge for its gift of allowing him to hide from the world while he reevaluated his life. If he had his way, he'd never return to reality at all.

Brayden backed his truck out of his garage, cringing at the mess Ed had left behind. The wreath he bought from Ava's store was murdered. Branches and fake berries lay strewn in the freshly fallen snow.

"Guess I'll have to get another," he murmured, shifting into park and hopping out.

He gathered up the mess and dropped it into the trash can as Elsie watched him from the window above. Normally, he brought her along for his deliveries, but today, he wasn't sure how long he'd be. He had extra errands to run before Ava was due to return, and he didn't want to leave his pup alone in the truck too long.

Ed's evidence of destruction cleaned up, Brayden moved the truck around to the shed to load up the bookshelf he finished last night for Sophie Grant.

He didn't need the money from his woodworking projects. Probably one of the reasons he kept his prices competitively low. But he enjoyed the creation process, one his grandpa taught him from a young age. It allowed him to escape reality more than the thousands of miles he'd traveled to get away from it.

Bookshelf loaded and properly protected with heavy quilts, Brayden headed toward the Sunset Ridge Lodge to make the delivery. A smile replaced any unwelcome thoughts as the lodge came into view. Snow covered the grounds and the green metal roof, much as it had when he arrived last March.

More than nine months later, and he was still in Sunset Ridge. So much longer than he said he'd stay, but the accident had rattled him more than his grandpa's passing.

As Brayden worked to unload the bookshelf onto his dolly, flickers from the event that should've stolen his life flashed through his memory. The sharp curve covered in black ice, his truck sliding right through the guardrail as if it were no more than tin foil. The never-ending rolling. The truck bouncing like a battered rubber ball. The seat belt cutting into his shoulder so hard he bled.

He'd squeezed his eyes shut and prayed.

When the truck finally stopped, he was upside down in a shallow creek. He shouldn't have survived, but he walked away with hardly a scratch.

There had to be a reason he was spared. Something more meaningful than running a multi-million-dollar marketing firm. He thought he might find the answer here in Sunset Ridge, but nothing seemed clear yet. Only that he was running out of time to make up his mind.

Brayden utilized the ramp to the summertime restaurant patio and cut to the left toward the main entrance. Sophie Grant requested the bookshelf for the lodge last month, and he finished it a few days ahead of schedule. With Ava so keen on avoiding him these past couple of weeks, he'd spent extra hours in his shed filling as many orders before Christmas as he could.

"Is that what I think it is?" Sophie's kind voice echoed off the high ceiling, her eyes widening in anticipation.

"One bookshelf, as requested."

"I didn't expect it until January."

Brayden rolled the dolly via Sophie's instructions and eased the shelf off. "I'm a little ahead of schedule," he admitted, shimmying the shelf a few inches from the wall. "Merry Christmas."

"Merry Christmas indeed." Sophie helped unwrap the bookshelf, *ooh*ing and *aah*ing as each layer of plastic peeled away. "Brayden, this is beautiful!"

"Glad you like it."

"Like it? I love it!" She pulled her phone from her pocket and started snapping pictures. "The book club is going to flip."

The front door closed, drawing Brayden's attention from behind. He expected a guest or one of the other Whitmore sisters, and was surprised to find Ava, juggling three different sized baskets. He hurried to her side and relieved her of the largest basket, its wobbles matching each cautious step.

"Brayden, what are *you* doing here?"

"A simple thank you would've cut it," he teased, setting the green cellophane-wrapped basket on the coffee table and taking another from Ava.

"Thank you. Just didn't expect to see you—" But

then she spotted the bookcase Sophie was practically petting. "Oh, a delivery?"

"Yeah."

Ava placed the smallest basket wrapped in silver beside the others as she purposefully looked Brayden up and down. Her raised eyebrow always did him in. Or maybe it was the way her lips lifted in one corner. "You put on pants," she noted in mock surprise.

"I even took that shower. Mark this day on your calendar."

Her eyes sparkled with her laugh, or maybe it was the reflection of Christmas lights from the massive tree in the center of the lobby. "I'm impressed."

There'd been a time when Brayden thought he and Ava might become an item. Their friendship had blossomed, and he worked up the courage to ask her out on a proper date. It took four tries before she finally agreed. But back then, he spent most nights working in his shed until early morning—he blamed the midnight sun—and embarrassingly had fallen asleep until well after the date was over. The next morning, he showed up at the store with coffee and donuts, but Ava wasn't having any of it.

She insisted they were better off as friends, and the botched date was a reminder of the time she didn't have for such things. Seemed she thought his falling asleep was excuse to flake, and he couldn't convince her otherwise. Their friendship never picked up where it left off. If it weren't for Elsie, Ava probably would've stopped talking to him entirely.

Though Brayden knew better than to hope this fake relationship might open a real door, a small part of him did anyway.

"Ava!" Cadence Whitmore—soon to be Harris—called from the kitchen doorway. "I was hoping you'd stop by today. I have something for you. I'll be right back."

Ava nodded, doing her best to avoid his gaze. It only offered him the opportunity for his eyes to linger a little longer. Ava Monroe was an incredibly attractive woman. It wasn't just her gentle brown eyes, or the way the sun illuminated the golden streaks in her dark hair. It was everything about her. Her laugh, her determination, her sweet nature.

Ava busied herself with the poufy red ribbon on the smallest basket.

"What are *you* doing here?" Brayden asked, turning his attention to the assortment of baskets. Each was a different size, all filled with Alaskan goodies. Many he recognized from her store—small Alaskan coffee packets, northern lights ornaments, and an assortment of fudge made in Fairbanks. Each basket was adorned with beautiful holiday ribbon and a giant bow.

"Trying something new."

"Ava, have you seen this bookshelf? Your neighbor is so talented!" Sophie cooed. "The book club will love it. And the best part? The guests will always feel welcome to join in on any current discussion."

"Clever idea," Ava complimented. "Leave extra copies of the books out here for them to browse—"

"You got it." Sophie looked back and forth between the two of them. "You two should join!"

"Oh, I don't have time to read," Ava said.

Sophie's eyes fell on Brayden, forcing an answer from him. "Maybe after the holidays." He nodded at the bookcase. "Lots of orders still to fill."

"Well, there's always room if either of you change your mind."

"Here you go," Cadence said to Ava, shoving an envelope at her. "I know it's short notice, but Ford and I hope you can come."

Brayden raised an eyebrow, certain the envelope contained a wedding invitation. As kind as the Whit-more sisters were to him when he arrived, he'd been too distant since then to earn an invitation. He liked

Ford Harris, but Brayden hadn't spent much time getting to know him as more than a passing acquaintance. When Brayden thought about it, the only true friend he'd made in Sunset Ridge was the hardware store owner, Harold Davies. *And Ava, once upon a time.*

"I better grab you a check," Sophie said to Brayden. "Be right back."

"A Christmas wedding?" Ava's eyes illuminated.

"Two days before Christmas, so we don't intrude too much on anyone's holiday plans. Besides the fact my sisters are relentless in reminding me that I was the first of us to actually get engaged but the last to tie the knot, we want to make sure Rilee can make it. She has a summer internship next year, so we decided to stop waiting."

"I have an interview with Rilee later," Ava said. "I'll be sure to give her that day off."

"Wonderful! Bring a plus-one if you like." Cadence briefly glanced at Brayden, her lips parted as if she were about to say more, but a ringing phone drew her away. She held up a finger. "Two minutes."

Ava folded her arms, then unfolded them and shoved both hands in her pockets. He wondered what she had to be nervous about. Surely a gentle insinuation that she bring him as a plus-one didn't have her all jittery. Their *virtual* fake relationship wouldn't require him to attend.

"What's with the baskets?" he asked when they were alone.

"Side project for the store," she answered without looking at him.

Brayden knelt down, taking special interest in them. The attention to detail, from the ribbon to the way each Alaskan-made item was nestled inside, was exquisite. These weren't simply baskets thrown together without care and precision. "This is what's in your garage, then?"

"Yes."

He hated how clipped her answers were and wished he could fix the awkward tension between them. Even if their fake relationship was only virtual, they still had to put on smiles and sit close together for some sweater deal. He wanted her to be comfortable around him. *It's still that letter, isn't it, Ava?* "Hey, why don't we grab those pictures now?" When she hesitated, he added, "I'm not wearing pajamas, and I don't know how long that'll last."

Ava cracked the faintest smile. "Fine, but make it quick." She shed her coat and waited for him to do the same. "I have a sales pitch to do."

The pieces fell together. Ava was here to

convince the Whitmore sisters to offer gift baskets to their guests. He wished he could stay to help. Sales pitches were a specialty of his, and these baskets would be an easy sell.

"I'm ready," Ava said.

Brayden was no selfie master, but he stood next to Ava and extended his arm above them as if he knew what he was doing. Though he possessed a wealth of social media knowledge for marketing purposes, he wasn't very good at anything personal.

"You're horrible at this," Ava ribbed. "Give it here."

"Your arms are too short," he countered.

"Well, at least point the phone down." She shimmied closer. "And put your arm around me like you actually *like* me or it'll never work."

Ava's peppermint scent drifted around him like an intoxicatingly euphoric cloud, momentarily causing him to forget what they were doing until she bumped him with her elbow. "I'll take a few," he said. "Now, smile like you don't hate me."

"I don't hate you."

Brayden snapped a few pictures. "Oh, really?"

"Really."

After a dozen clicks, footsteps forced them apart, but her peppermint scent lingered on his shirt. He quickly scrolled through the pictures when Sophie was detained by a guest with a question.

"Any good?" Ava asked, leaning over his arm to see.

He angled his phone better for her to see. "This one should work." He'd chosen the picture that best captured her dazzling smile and that hint of playfulness when she insisted she didn't hate him.

"Good, send it to me. My mom has taken it upon herself to set me up on a date with some guy named Pete and without this, I'm not getting out of it." She stepped away the moment he hit send, pretending to fuss with her already perfect baskets.

"Here you go," Sophie said, handing him a check. "I still don't think it's enough."

"It's plenty," he said, folding and stuffing it into a shirt pocket. "I hope your book club enjoys it."

"Remember, the invitation is still open to join."

Brayden nodded. His gaze inevitably fell on Ava as she launched into her spiel with Cadence over the baskets, his cue to leave before he did something foolish like intervene without an invitation. He could help in other ways. Like notifying his property manager to order a basket for each of his tenants once Ava officially announced they were for sale.

For now, he had an appointment with the local

realtor about another property. One that needed a bit more work than some of the previous houses he'd bought. But the location promised it was worth every penny. In the end, the community would benefit the most. He'd been buying properties in poor condition and having them flipped all year long. His way of giving back to a town that had provided him such peace of mind.

He sat inside his truck, giving it a moment to warm back up. Mom had another half dozen text messages waiting for him, this time about missed opportunities and some woman she'd wanted him to marry being engaged to someone else.

Brayden: I've met someone.

He included his favorite picture with Ava in the message before silencing his phone and backing out of the gravel drive. He drove through town feeling lighter. Maybe he couldn't shirk his business responsibilities forever, but at least Mom should stop trying to arrange him in a marriage he didn't want.

Parking on the curb in front of the town's newest listing, Brayden meant to notify Jolene he was there for the showing. But Mom's name flashed on the screen. *She's quick.*

Mom: I'm not amused.

Brayden: Careful. We might elope ;)

Mom: You can't be serious about her.

Brayden: Deadly

A few ominous minutes elapsed as he waited in the truck. When Jolene Davies pulled up behind him, his phone buzzed once more.

Mom: I'm coming to Alaska. Be there Friday.

Chapter Three

AVA

"You didn't tell me you were dating Brayden Young!" Kinley James burst into the Forget Me Not Boutique and marched straight to the counter, pinning Ava in an uncomfortable stare. Her best friend's eyes were much too bright and her smile three times the size it should be. *This can't be good.*

"You're finally seeing that handsome young neighbor of yours?" Glenda cooed, clapping her hands together. The older woman, who reminded Ava a lot of her grandmother, wasn't due to arrive for her shift for another hour but found herself unable to sit still at home. Any other day, Ava would've been grateful.

"Brayden Young?" Becca, the teenager who worked odd shifts around her school schedule, chimed in. Ava felt sabotaged by everyone currently in her store. "He's so dreamy!"

"What are you all talking about?" Ava asked with a raised eyebrow, doing her best to remain cool on the outside. Inside, her heart beat wildly with fear. She hadn't had time to fill Kinley in on the fake relationship. She was planning to mention it tomorrow when they met for lunch to talk brides-maid dresses. "I'm not dating him." A few giggles followed, forcing Ava to repeat herself. "I'm *not*."

Kinley leaned against the counter, that mischie-vous twinkle in her eyes as she scrolled through her phone. "Here it is." She held it up for Ava to see the screen.

Ava's eyes tripled in size as the photo she and Brayden took only a couple of hours ago stared back at her. One she had sent to only one person. "Where did you find that?"

"Your mom's Facebook page."

The color drained from Ava's face as she realized the single photo she'd sent her mom was now posted on social media with dozens of heart emojis. Mom had *way* too many friends. Way too many *local* friends. Her post, hardly an hour old, already had over fifty interactions and dozens of comments. Ava recognized far too many names. *Should've just gone on the date.*

She dropped her elbows on the counter and covered her face with both hands. *Deep breaths.* "This is a disaster."

Three expectant sets of eyes fixated on her. For once, Ava was relieved the store was empty of customers. Not that they'd be alone for long. She suspected more than a few locals would pop by to pry into her love life. *Well, they'd better buy something too.* "It's a . . . long story."

"So, are you, then?" Kinley pressed.

Ava spent too long selecting words in her head. Before she could get any of them out, her phone buzzed beside her. She didn't have to look at the screen to know who it was. After dozens of ignored texts, Mom was back to calling.

As tempting as it was to send her to voicemail and crawl into a dark hole until this all blew over, she was too furious about the invasion of privacy. "Give me a minute." She swiped her phone off the counter and barricaded herself in her office, away from prying ears. After a breath so deep she thought she might pass out, she hit the answer button.

"Ava, I'm so happy for you!"

"Mom, take it down. You had no right."

"Oh, come on. You can't send me such an adorable picture and expect me to keep it a secret. Especially when Mary Ellis's daughter just announced she's having twins. That boy is pretty cute, Ava dear. How long have you been keeping him a secret from me?"

Ava groaned and dropped into a chair. Maybe this whole thing was stupid. If she'd only thought it through for twenty-four hours, she'd never have agreed. Common sense would've warned her where this might lead. Why did she let Brayden talk her into this? How would she explain to an entire town that this was just a hoax? "That was a private photo. It wasn't yours to share with the whole world, Mom."

"I'm sorry, dear. I was just so happy you finally met someone. And he's so dishy, too!"

"Can you *please* take it down?" Ava asked through gritted teeth, working to calm her erratically beating heart in a futile attempt at multitasking. So much for spending time at the shop today. The moment she was finished with Rilee's interview, she'd have to head straight home and warn Brayden of the impending doom. He could hide out in his shop until the holidays were over. Or at least until Cadence's wedding. The town generally forgot level-one dating when a wedding was on the horizon.

Ava dropped her forehead into the palm of one hand, phone still pressed to her ear. She couldn't abandon the store, though the temptation to hunker down at home in pajamas for a couple of weeks sounded nice.

"I don't know how to do that. I'm still learning, you see."

Mom, you are such a terrible liar. Ava swore she could hear the giggle in her mom's voice. "Have Jamie show you. You're over at her house, right?"

"She ran to Target. I'm hanging out with Trey. Ava dear, are you sure I can't leave it up? It's such a cute photo. I can tell from those eyes that he looks like a keeper. I know Pete will be devastated once he sees it, but I'm sure he'll understand. It might help lessen the blow."

"Pete?"

"Geraldine Franks' grandson."

Right. The setup. How could I forget the bullet I barely dodged? "He'll be fine, Mom. Take it down."

"I'll talk to your sister when she gets back." Mom cleared her throat, and Ava held her breath, awaiting

43

whatever question came next. "How's the store? Did you get all the decorations up for Christmas? Run all the holidays sales? I thought you underpriced those angel ornaments. You should mark them up a dollar."

Ava pressed her palm against her forehead a little harder, pretending she could rub away the growing headache. This was why she sent most of Mom's calls to voicemail. To avoid *this* conversation. After she figured out how to get off the phone with her lovingly overbearing mother, she was going to blackmail Jamie into getting that photo off social media, like yesterday. "Fine, Mom. Everything is fine. All is on schedule."

"I didn't see the buy-three-get-one-free fudge sale mentioned on the website."

"I'm not running that one this year. Switching it up."

"That's a shame. Was always one of my best sales."

And my worst last Christmas. "Did you need something else?"

"I'm surprised you answered," she continued. "It's usually so busy this time of year. I remember working fourteen-hour days and forgetting all about lunch. If Chase didn't cook dinner some of those nights when your dad was working late too, you all would've starved. There simply wasn't time for me to do it and keep up."

"I'm working on the schedule." Ava opened her planner to the scheduling page, just so she wasn't telling a complete lie. Her meticulously color-coded system stared back at her. "Glenda and Becca have things covered out front for now. Plus, I'm interviewing Rilee Harris in half an hour. She's going to take some shifts while she's home for Christmas."

"Is that in your budget?"

No. "Don't worry about that, Mom. You're retired, remember?" When Ava decided to go all-in on her customized Christmas basket idea, she left only enough money in her business account to cover her employee expenses. If she was forced to close her doors on Christmas Eve, she wouldn't send anyone away without full compensation. Including Rilee.

Hopefully, it wouldn't come to that. Though the Whitmore sisters hadn't given her a concrete yes, their maybe was promising.

"I want the store to be a success for you, Ava. And for your daughter someday."

Time to change the subject. "How's Jamie?" Ava wasn't as close to her little sister as she was to Chase. Most of her updates about Jamie and her family came from Mom. Those were the texts she actually welcomed, especially the ones with pictures of her four-year-old nephew, Trey. "Everything going well with her pregnancy?"

"Oh, yes! The doctor is quite pleased. The baby is healthy and everything is right on track. So much calmer this time around."

"That's good." Ava shuffled through the mess on her desk, embarrassed she'd let things get so out of hand. She didn't want Rilee to panic and run before she ever got started, so she cleaned things up, hoping to also make peace with her mom before the conversation ended.

"How serious are things with this Bradley?" Mom pried.

"Brayden."

"Brayden," Mom repeated. "Is there a ring in your future?"

"Mom!"

"It's a fair question." When Ava didn't offer up an answer, Mom continued. "Is he from Alaska? Has he been married before? Any kids?"

"Mom, I'm twenty-eight, not dead. There are still single, never-been-married-before men my age." She couldn't say for sure Brayden was one of them, only that she thought he was. She gave up organizing the chaos on her desk and instead scooped it all into a box she promptly shoved under her desk. "We'll talk about him later, okay? Just get that picture down before the whole town sees it."

"Just one more thing, honey."

"Yes?"

"I thought it was time I came and spent Christmas with you and Chase. Meet your new beau."

Ava was thankful her coffee cup was empty. She'd have choked on it. "You can't leave Jamie alone this year. She's about to pop. And what about Trey? You don't want to miss Christmas with your *only* grandkid."

"Jamie's fine, dear. It's baby number two. It's all downhill from here. She doesn't need me hovering. And Trey is already excited about Skyping with Grandma this year. I talked to him all about it."

This sounded . . . ominous.

"Mom, it's fine. You don't need to come. I'll be busy with the store. Chase, well, you know how he is."

"Too late."

"What?"

"I already booked the ticket. Chose that nonrefundable option because it's so much cheaper, you know. I'll be in Anchorage Friday morning. I'll get

Chase to pick me up from the airport. I'm sure you'll be much too busy with the store."

Ava felt what color remained drain from her face. This couldn't be happening. Things were already bad enough with Mom meddling in her life. Brayden would probably run far, far away when he discovered what a mess her family had created for him. She wouldn't even blame him. And the store. How on earth was she supposed to keep the imminent demise of the store a secret over the holidays with Mom in physical proximity to snoop? The bank would post their foreclosure notice on Christmas Day if she didn't pull this off.

This was a disaster.

"I'll email you my itinerary," Mom added.

Ava didn't have any words left as she sank into her chair and tried not to slither to the floor.

"Oh, Jamie's back!"

"The picture—"

"I'll see you Friday, honey. We can grab dinner. I've been dying to try that new lodge restaurant." The phone went silent seconds before a knock on her office door forced her to recover. Through the slivers of glass not covered by a giant holiday wreath, she spotted Rilee Harris.

"Just a minute!" she called, hoping Rilee was

available to start today. She'd need all the help she could get if she was going to save the store and survive her mom in town. She also had to figure out what to say to the lurkers outside her office door about this relationship. But first she sent an SOS text to Brayden. They'd need coffee. Lots of coffee.

"I got here as fast as I could," Brayden said, appearing at the top of her stairs with Elsie at his heel and two raised coffees in offering. His widened eyes were no doubt caused by the alarming amount of Christmas chaos spread throughout her living room. "What are you doing?"

"Panic decorating." Ava set the box of ornaments she'd been holding onto a precariously tall stack of others. Still panting heavily from her countless trips up and the down the stairs, she glanced around the room. "What does it look like I'm doing?" She accepted the cup from Black Bear Coffee as he moved into the living room and Elsie sniffed at the boxes. "Peppermint. Good choice."

"Why?"

"Because peppermint and Christmas go together?"

"No, I meant the decorating. You went from zero to a hundred pretty quickly."

Pushing hair out of her eyes, she focused on steadying her breathing. "I don't know how to say this, so I'm just going to come out with it." Buying herself a few seconds to work up her courage, Ava sipped her latte and watched Elsie saunter to the window. "My mom's coming to town. Friday afternoon."

Brayden laughed, slow and quiet at first. But he didn't stop. Instead, his laughter built until Elsie wagged her tail in curiosity. Ava might've enjoyed the sound of his deep, warm chortle if it weren't so ominous.

"This is *funny* to you?"

"Oh, yeah. It's . . . well, I shouldn't even be surprised."

"This is your fault. Do you have any idea what you've done? Or what you're in for, I might add? My mom is *from* Sunset Ridge and used to run the store. She knows the entire town. Just because she moved away doesn't mean she lost contact with a single person. Stupid social media."

Brayden took a leisurely sip of his coffee, no urgency in anything he did. How could the man be calm in a situation that demanded panic? "Well, you're not the only one with a major dilemma caused by our brilliant idea."

"*Our?*" Ava shook her head, waving Brayden along downstairs. At least a dozen boxes and totes still needed to make their way upstairs, and she was putting him to work as punishment. "Oh, no. This was your idea. I was joking. You ran with it. Your trigger finger took those selfies that sealed our fate."

"You agreed."

Ava shoved a tote at Brayden, then grabbed one for herself. They carried them upstairs. Elsie was content to be the lookout at the window as they made decoration runs. "My mom posted our picture on Facebook. The whole town will think we're a hot item by sundown. Oh, and she's so happy I'm not hopelessly single that she's coming to *meet* you."

Brayden beat her downstairs and grabbed two more totes. "Huh, isn't that something."

"That's all you have to say about this?"

"Friday, you said?"

"Yeah."

"Some timing," he mumbled.

"Oh, is that inconvenient for you?"

"My mom's arriving on Friday, too."

Ava nearly dropped a tote filled with lights on her slipper-clad toes. "You're kidding."

"Afraid not." Brayden scanned the living room. "*All* of these are filled with Christmas decorations?"

"Yep."

"Why do you need so many?"

Ava retreated downstairs and together they secured the last of the Christmas decorations. "You should know something about my mom. There's nothing she loves more than Christmas. I mean, I'm pretty sure she loves the holiday more than she loves her own kids. If she showed up and I had nothing up, it'd be worse than her finding out this whole relationship thing is a scam. So much worse." Ava left out that an undecorated house would tip her mom off that the store was in peril. She couldn't have that.

"Worse than being forced out on a date with Pete?"

"I haven't decided." But Ava finally managed to let out a chuckle. The first one in hours. "How are you so much calmer than I am?"

Brayden shrugged. "I guess all my panic is inward. My mother isn't going to approve of you, but that's not unexpected."

"Why won't she like me?" Ava reached for her coffee and took a generous gulp now that it'd cooled. "I happen to think I'm pretty great, you know. Or is this one of those *no one is ever going to be good enough for her baby* things?"

"She didn't pick you," Brayden explained. "But it's more."

"More?"

Brayden nodded, turning his attention toward the stacks of holiday boxes.

"There you go again with the vague explanations," Ava mumbled. "That's your single most annoying quality, did you know that?"

"Look at us, going at it like an old married couple already. We should be able to pull this off without a hitch. Unless you want to back out?"

"Two words. Nonrefundable ticket." It wasn't lost on Ava how easily Brayden skirted her prying. He was a master at it, but she had more important things to worry about than Brayden's mysteriousness. Like getting all of these decorations out and up. Starting with the tree she'd meant to replace for years. "I'm not backing out. And neither are you. You'll be the only true buffer I have from my mom. Your most important job is to keep her nose out of my store business."

"What about your brother? Or your friend who's engaged? Can't they help?"

"Kinley's elbow-deep in wedding plans. I'm not

troubling her with this. And Chase, he's way too amused to be reliable." Ava pulled a thin tree from its box, horrorstruck by its pitiful nature. *Worse than I thought.* She'd been meaning to get a new tree for the past three years. But there'd never been time.

"You're not seriously putting up a Charlie Brown tree, are you?"

"It's not—"

Elsie let out a loud bark from the window.

"Squirrel."

"It's bad, isn't it?" Ava asked. "The tree?"

"My mom won't like you, and there's not much I can do to help you there."

"That seems like quite the disadvantage," Ava cut in. "But what does that have to do with my tree?"

"Trust me, if you *were* the type she approved of, I never would've asked you out on that date." Brayden didn't give Ava time to do more than blush before he went on. "But if you put up that tree, she might have a heart attack. From the sound of it, your mom might too." Brayden grabbed her wrist and pulled her toward the stairs. "We have to get you a different tree."

"Now?"

"We have less than forty-eight hours before our mothers descend on our lives. It's go time." Brayden waited for her at the front door, shrugging into his coat. How could she tell him she couldn't afford a new tree without the whole dire money situation coming up? Whether he knew the truth or not, now was not the moment she wanted to have that humiliating discussion. Maybe Harold would let her put it on a tab. *Just this once.*

"If we're going to the hardware store—the only place in town that sells trees—I'm bringing one of my Christmas baskets. Elsie can stay here. I don't mind."

"I'll get the truck out."

Ava waited for Brayden to close the front door behind him before she released a deep breath. This was a mess. This whole thing was nuts. If they'd just stuck to sending overbearing parents to voicemail, none of this would be happening. Now she had to survive not only *her* mother but another one doomed to hate her on principle?

"Elsie, I don't think there's a Christmas miracle big enough for this year."

Chapter Four

Brayden

During his time in Sunset Ridge, Brayden had become intimately familiar with Davies Hardware store. He might even dare to call the owner, Harold, a friend. When it came to his woodworking supplies, Brayden shopped local when he could and only made the occasional trip to Anchorage when the local hardware store wasn't able to order what he needed.

When Brayden's corporate career gained momentum, he lost sight of small places like this store. Places his grandpa swore by. He stuck to convenience when he had time to shop at all. But living in the small town for over nine months reminded him of who he always wanted to be. Someone who gave back, like Grandpa had.

Brayden welcomed the clamor of bells as he held the door open for Ava.

"Are you paying for this?" Ava meant the words as a tease, he was sure. But he knew the truth. She couldn't afford a new tree. Especially not the biggest one Harold had to offer, which was the only one he was allowing her to leave with.

"Of course I'm paying for it. As you said, I got you into this mess, right?"

"I was joking."

Brayden steered a shopping cart straight toward the tree display, waving to Harold at the front counter on his way. The older man had his head tucked into a newspaper, no doubt working on the crossword puzzle. "And because I'm paying, you have to accept the one I choose."

"That not's fair."

"I think it's entirely fair. I don't have my own tree, so this one has to count for the two of us." He scanned the shelves below the display of five artificial trees for the box he sought. The selection that included a three-footer, a super skinny six-footer, and the lush seven-and-a-half-foot cashmere tree he wanted was quite picked through and the remaining boxes weren't in any order.

Ava shifted the holiday basket she'd brought with her from one hand to the other, making him wonder what goodies might be in there he couldn't see for it to tire her arm out. "My living room isn't *that* big."

"It's big enough." Brayden hefted the last remaining box of the biggest tree into the cart and looked toward a skimpy ornament display. "You're good on decorations, right?"

"In case you missed how Christmas exploded in my house, I have enough ornaments to decorate three trees this size. The lights on the other hand . . ."

"Point taken." He steered toward the endcap filled with boxes of colorful lights and began loading them into the cart. "We don't have time to fix old strands." After the sixth or seventh box, Ava shackled his wrist.

"That's plenty."

He stared too long as her slender fingers wrapped around his wrist, surprised by the tingles erupting on his exposed skin. "Better get this to the register, then. I think Harold's about due for a coffee break." He nodded toward the owner shrugging into a jacket. Either the crossword puzzle was finished or he was stumped and needed a break.

He snagged a bucket of wood screws on the way to the counter.

"Brayden," Harold greeted with a warm smile. Crinkle lines around his eyes and more gray hair than not suggested he was a few years older than Brayden's mom. Not quite old enough to be his grandfather, but Harold reminded him of one anyway. "Not your usual haul today, aside from the screws, of course."

"Tree emergency."

"I see that." Harold flashed a smile toward Ava.

"Mr. Davies, how are you?" Ava returned a friendly smile and lifted her gift basket onto the counter. "I was wondering if I could ask a small favor. I'm offering these gift baskets in my store. They're kind of a last-minute addition. Would you mind displaying one on your counter?"

Harold studied the basket with interest. "You put this together yourself?"

"I did." Brayden didn't miss how she rocked on her heels. The gravity of these baskets occurred to him. Was it possible that they were the hopeful ace up her sleeve? Her last-ditch effort to raise enough money to save the store?

"They make wonderful holiday gifts," Brayden added.

"It's just a display," Ava continued. "You can send customers to my store to buy them so you don't have to fuss with any of that." Her arm disappeared up to the elbow into her tote she called a purse. "I have multiple sizes." She handed him a printed card showcasing the three sizes and prices.

It took all of Brayden's discipline not to critique the design aloud. Her website wasn't listed, for one. And half a dozen more eye-catching designs arranged themselves in his head. He only hoped she hadn't already printed hundreds. He'd risk wounding her pride this once and offer to redo them.

"I don't see the harm," Harold said, clearing a spot on the long counter for the basket. "Don't know how much business it'll send your way though."

"Thank you, Mr. Davies."

Brayden expected Ava to do more or say more, but instead she waited quietly as he paid. It was so unlike her that he could hardly concentrate on signing the receipt. Ava was far from what he would consider shy. It had to be something else. "Harold, your wife's a realtor, right?"

"Yes." A knowing twinkle danced in Harold's eyes. Brayden had suspected for a long time that Harold knew the truth about him. It would be hard to be married to a realtor in a small town and not wonder where all the extra commission checks came from. But the man didn't give him away if he did know.

"Those baskets might make nice client gifts," Brayden said. "Especially for new homeowners."

"Great idea," Harold said with a nod, handing Brayden the receipt. "I'll mention it to Jolene."

"She can contact me if interested," Ava added as the three moved to the front of the store, Harold at their side to lock up and seek out a cup of coffee. "I should have them added to my website later tonight."

Before they could make it to the front door, bells jingled overhead. An elderly woman with a red hat and snow boots up to the hem of her calf-length skirt marched in. She was a petite thing, and Brayden was certain he'd seen her around before. But hiding out in a woodworking shop more days than not had its disadvantages. He couldn't place her name.

"Aren't you two just the cutest couple!" the woman cooed.

Ava's eyes doubled in size. "Hi, Mrs. Franks."

Geraldine latched on to Brayden's arm, her grip surprisingly strong. "My poor Pete is crushed about the date, but well, when your mother asked me to set it up, we had no idea this secret romance was blossoming all along!"

Brayden bit down on his bottom lip to keep from bursting out with laughter at Ava's obvious mortification. Harold's eyebrow was raised, but he kept quiet. Brayden might hear his real thoughts the next time he stopped in for stain or saw blades.

"You talked to my mom," Ava said, her words a statement and not a question.

"Saw the picture on that book face thingy. You know, that Internet site."

Ava forced a smile. "Of course you did."

Brayden managed to swallow the brunt of his laughter so he could swoop in before the conversation became too awkward. "I don't believe I've had the pleasure," he directed at Mrs. Franks. "I'm Brayden Young."

"Geraldine Franks." She shook his hand, her eyes sparkling with excitement. He now understood Ava's panic a little more. How long before the entire town decided they were an item? Sundown might not be an exaggeration, and with the darker winter days, that wasn't but a couple of hours away. He should be irritated at the invasion of privacy, but he wasn't. *Odd.*

"Pleasure to meet you," Brayden added. "Sorry about Pete."

"We better be going, right, *honey*?" Ava yanked

on his arm, hard enough to rock him off his steady footing. "Tree to decorate and all before Mom gets here."

"Merry Christmas, Mrs. Franks," Brayden added with a wave as Ava yanked him outside. Once the glass door fell closed behind them and Geraldine turned her attention to Harold, Ava's eyes narrowed at him like daggers. He ignored the scary look as he loaded the tree into the back of his truck.

"This is a nightmare."

"Oh, come on. It's not *that* bad," he said, meaning it. "So the town thinks we're dating. Won't that be a little easier in the whole convincing-our-moms thing since they're coming here now?"

"You don't get it, do you?"

"Get what?" Brayden placed the sack of lights in the back seat and closed the door as another truck pulled in beside them.

"Great," Ava muttered. "Just what I need today."

Chase Monroe stepped out of the truck, a cheeky grin already on his face. Brayden had only started to scratch the surface of conversation where Ava's family was concerned before that dreadful day when he missed their date. She'd closed up after that, so he had no idea what to expect of her brother. Whether or not he was the protective type. But judging by his expression, he not only had seen the photo for himself, but was quite amused.

"You two, huh?" Chase looked back and forth between them with a mischievous smirk.

"No," Ava corrected so quickly it actually stung a bit. "I was trying to get Mom off my back. This whole thing is fake. She wasn't supposed to post that stupid photo. She definitely wasn't supposed to get on a plane to Alaska. This is one big mess."

Chase let out a laugh. "Doesn't look so fake online. It's everywhere now."

Ava snatched the phone from Chase. "Thirty-nine shares? What the jingle bells? She was supposed to take it down. I'm going to kill Jamie."

"It's Christmas," Chase said, unable to finish without laughing.

"I don't care. She was supposed to help Mom make it go away. I knew I should've kept that seventh-grade school photo. All my blackmail is gone, and she knows it."

"Yeah, I doubt she's going to help you out. She's having too much fun with the comments." Chase pried his phone from Ava's clenched fingers and dropped it in a coat pocket. "Mom's coming to town whether you two like it or not. Cheer up. It won't be so bad."

"Easy for you to say." Ava let out a heavy sigh. "Look, I need you to pretend this is legit. Don't go giving us away during the Christmas sweater party. I can't go back on any of this now, or I'll ruin Christmas."

Brayden laughed. "Dramatic much?"

"You don't know our mom," Chase chimed in, his tone serious this time. "Look, I'll keep your secret. It works in my favor as Mom's finally off my case about grandkids. Guess you could say I got my gift early this year."

"Ha ha." Ava shoved her gloveless hands into her coat pockets, and Brayden fought the urge to put his arm around her to keep her warm. He took a step away to keep from acting on the impulse that would be hard to explain to the one person who knew this was a sham. "You're picking her up from the airport, right?"

"Nope," Chase answered. "Decided she wanted to rent a big SUV and drive herself."

"Decided or was persuaded?" Ava asked.

"I didn't volunteer you, so you're welcome."

"A lot of help you are," Ava muttered. "That makes her completely mobile. C'mon, Brayden. We need to get that tree up."

"Be sure to post pictures for Mom to share with

two hundred of her closest friends," Chase hollered from the sidewalk. "And Brayden?"

Brayden braced for the older brother's warning finally headed his way. "Yeah?"

"Get a Christmas sweater. If you want to know the key to Mom's heart, get one with cats."

"Cats?" Brayden repeated as Chase entered the hardware store. He looked at Ava. "Your mom is a cat person?"

"That's not really the biggest problem we have right now, is it?" Ava hopped into the truck and slammed the door shut, waiting for him to do the same.

Ava seemed extra rattled as Brayden drove through the downtown strip. Had they not both had their fill of coffee for the day, he'd offer to stop and get more. But his stomach demanded sustenance, and more coffee might make them both more jittery. "I can order something from Warren's," he said, turning into their shared driveway.

"If you're expecting me to turn that down, you made the wrong offer." A hint of a twinkle danced in her eyes before it fled. He yearned to reach out and touch her hand. To reassure her that no matter the mess they created, they'd be okay. Cat Christmas sweaters and all. Maybe he wasn't her favorite person, but he certainly wasn't her enemy.

"I'll call in an order once I let Elsie out."

"You don't have to help with the tree—"

"Of course I do." Brayden backed up to her side of the duplex and hopped out to unload before she could object. He had a couple of orders to finish before Christmas, and one of them was hardly started. But it felt wrong to abandon Ava now. He was no stranger to working through the night. He'd actually grown rather fond of watching the northern lights out the shed window as he worked. A few more late nights wouldn't kill him. "We're in this together now."

Ava stared at him a moment longer than he could handle. His pulse doubled, then tripled, forcing him to look away from her soft lips. How many times had he imagined kissing her? Would they have to kiss to convince their moms this was real? Secretly, he hoped so. Maybe he should plant some mistletoe to ensure it. He pushed open his door, breaking the spell. "Let's get the tree inside."

He hefted the box up the concrete stairs, watching Elsie from the window as Ava unlocked the door. "I've never had a dog until I moved here," he said, carrying the box into the living room, the pup's tail wagging in earnest curiosity.

"Really? Not even when you were a kid?"

"Dad always wanted one, but Mom put her foot down pretty firmly. Said they were too much responsibility and we were never home enough." He laid the box down so it'd be easy to bust open. Elsie sniffed at the package with rapt interest. "Needless to say, my mom won't be overly thrilled with Elsie." *If she stays long enough to meet her.*

Ava slipped into the kitchen, opening a cupboard. "Who could *not* immediately fall in love with this bundle of adorable fur? She's perfect in every way." She knelt down and offered the golden a treat. "Aren't you, girl?"

The sight melted his heart, reminding him why he fell for Ava all those months ago. Maybe, forced together as they would be with this fake relationship, they could repair their fractured friendship. Even if Brayden never got a real first date out of Ava, he missed the friend he made when she first moved in next door.

"Halibut tacos sound good to you?" he asked once Ava cut open the tree box.

Her eyes sparkled. "They sound like the best thing about today."

"C'mon, Elsie," he called from the sliding-glass door. "Time to go outside." He turned back to Ava. She didn't waste a minute getting to work unpacking the various branches and piling them along the floor.

"Ava?"

"Yeah?"

He wanted to reassure her everything would work out. That they would survive this holiday season together. More than anything, he wanted to gather her into his arms and promise to help her through this bump in the road—the whole bump. The confession that he read her letter after all lodged in his throat. But she was only tolerating him because their simple plan backfired. If it wasn't for Ed, she would still be avoiding him.

"What do you want to drink?" he asked instead.

"Dr. Pepper."

"You got it." He lingered a moment more, but the words didn't come. He welcomed the cold air on the deck as he shuffled through the snow-covered planks to watch Elsie trot happily through the snow below.

Brayden pulled out his phone to call in their food order, but instead dialed his sister. He hadn't spoken to Sarra in a few weeks, and he felt guilty about that. She'd sent him a text two days ago, asking him to call her when he got a chance, but he'd put it off. He'd forgotten all about it until he caught a glimpse of red garland falling out of a bag in Ava's living room moments ago. It reminded him of family Christmases before Dad passed.

"Brayden, hi."

"How's my baby sister?"

"Oh, you know me. Busy as ever." The typical answer made Brayden frown. Maybe Ava had a point about his vague answers. He could hide behind excuses to keep a low profile in Sunset Ridge, but in truth, it was how his family operated. Especially after his father passed at a young age. "You must be busy too if it took you so long to call me."

"A little." He gave her several seconds to explain the need for the call, but when she didn't say anything, he bought her time. "How's your fiancé?"

"Your phone isn't tapped, is it?" she asked with an uneasy laugh.

"Relax. I'm on my deck, watching Elsie play in the snow. I haven't told anyone that you and Hunter are engaged, just like I promised. You get the pleasure of breaking *that* news to Mom yourself."

"Good. Because I have another secret I need you to keep."

Brayden kicked a chunk of ice, freeing it from the

deck planks. Sarra already secretly dated a man Mom didn't approve of. He wasn't sure what else it could be. *Unless* . . . "You know I won't say anything."

"Good. Because I'm accepting another job."

"And here I thought you were going to tell me you eloped."

Sarra let out a quick laugh. "No time for that. I'm accepting a VP position with her biggest competitor. I'm not telling Mom until after Christmas, and she won't be happy. But I've hit my ceiling with her company. I need bigger challenges. A sturdier ladder."

"She'll be hard-pressed to lose you."

"Will she?" Sarra countered. "She's been grooming you to run the company since you were old enough to have a job. You're the one with a corner office waiting."

"Yeah." Brayden shoved his free hand in his pocket and let out a heavy sigh. *An office I don't want anymore.*

"Brayden, everything okay?"

"Yeah."

"Liar."

With a few cautious steps, he peeked through the sliding-glass door into Ava's place, ensuring she was preoccupied with decorations. "Mom's coming to Alaska."

"That makes sense."

"It does?" Brayden regretted making this call outside. But Elsie was investigating a questionable tree branch poking out of the ground and he hated to spoil her excitement. "What aren't you telling me?"

"You don't know."

"What's to know? Mom's coming to meet Ava."

"Ava?" He gave Sarra a moment. "*The* Ava? You two worked things out?"

"No. Not exactly. It's . . . a long story."

Sarra laughed this time. "Aren't we something with our predictably vague responses?"

"Right."

"Brayden, I have something to tell you, and I don't think you'll like hearing it. But, well, you know how I hate surprises."

Brayden tensed, bracing for whatever upsetting news his sister was about to hit him with. "Everything okay with you? Hunter?"

"Everything is fine here," Sarra said, her voice sincere. "Mom's retiring."

"I know that. Two years."

"No. January first. Of *next* year."

Brayden's heart stopped cold, and he couldn't

even blame the wintery chill. January first bought him weeks. Days, really. "That can't be right."

"She's planning to announce it to the company at the Christmas party next week. And if she hasn't told *you* yet—"

"She's coming up here because she plans to bring me back with her." Brayden dug his fingers into the back of his neck. If Mom was retiring ahead of schedule, she'd expect him to take over right away. As Elsie trotted back up the stairs, he looked through the window and watched Ava dancing to Christmas music as she spread strands of lights on the couch. "That's not enough time."

"Mom and I still aren't on the best of speaking terms." She didn't have to say it, they both knew. *Because of Hunter.* Mom didn't think he was marriage material. Too many tattoos for her liking. "I'm not even supposed to know. She'd probably write me out of the will if she found out I told you, but I didn't want her to ambush you. Is there anything I can do?"

"No." Brayden leaned against the snow-covered railing, not caring that his forearms would be damp. He hadn't seen his sister since Grandpa's funeral. He missed her. At one time, they had flirted with the idea of Sarra and Hunter coming to Sunset Ridge to spend Christmas with him. "I have to figure this out for myself."

"I'm sorry, Brayden. But I thought it was only fair you knew before she blindsided you."

"Thank you." Elsie let out a series of barks as a bird fluttered away. "I better go."

"Brayden?"

"Yeah?"

"Good luck."

Brayden tried and failed to hide his heavy sigh, and simply said, "Thanks." He whistled for Elsie and ushered her inside his place to let his fingers thaw, call Warren's, and ward off a panic attack before he returned to Ava's. He wasn't ready to make the biggest decision of his life on such short notice, but what choice did he have?

Chapter Five

Ava

"If we're going to be a couple, you'll have to be a little more open about who you are," Ava said to Brayden as she shaped branches. The tree was beautiful—on the display rack. But the boxed version required a lot of work before a single decoration could be hung. At this rate, she'd be lucky to get lights on before midnight.

"What do you want to know?"

Ava peeked around from the back side of the tree. "That's too easy. You're going to tell me anything, just like that?"

"As you pointed out, we're a couple. Ask away."

Reaching for her fountain drink with a Warren's Sea Shack logo on the cup, Ava took a long sip of Dr. Pepper. He didn't promise to answer, but this was progress. She stole a second sip before setting the cup down. She rarely drank soda, but tonight she was making an exception. She needed all the caffeine she could get, and she was coffeed out. After the tree was decorated, she still had baskets to assemble for her store display. *So many baskets.* "You mentioned a sister once before. Do you have any other siblings?"

"Just the sister."

Ava purposely raised an eyebrow for Brayden to see. "It might help if I knew her name."

"Sarra."

"Older or younger?"

"Younger."

"Okay, now we're getting somewhere." Ava flexed her aching fingers, studying the remaining branches on her side that needed fluffing. *Too many.* One of the questions she most wanted to ask was whether he had read her final notice letter. But the atmosphere was much too light with the cheerful Christmas music, a goofy snoozing golden pawing at the air, and a stomach full of Warren's famous halibut tacos. Ava swallowed the question and chose another. "You two close? You and Sarra?"

"Depends what you mean by close."

It was impossible not to laugh, meeting the same roadblocks as every other conversation. "Were you in politics or something in your former life? You're great at evading questions, yet still making it sound like you're answering them."

"Not a chance." Brayden flashed her a smirk that made her stomach unexpectedly flutter. She ducked behind the safety of the tree. No, she would not get carried away when it came to Brayden Young. It was a fake relationship that they'd bust right open when their moms left or maybe once they stopped harassing them about grandkids. It was entirely possible the whole charade wouldn't last the weekend, much less through Christmas.

Those dangerous smirks were to be avoided at all costs. Nothing real would come from something so made up, and it was better that way.

Besides, Ava told herself, she still had a sour taste in her mouth over the date Brayden never made. One in which he claimed to have fallen asleep in his woodworking shed *and* misplaced his phone for several hours. He may as well have told her *something came up*. The excuses were equally lame and unbelievable. Ava recognized the tactic. A line like that had been used on her before.

As she sat alone at a corner table at Warren's that night, waiting for Brayden to show, she remembered why she avoided dating in the first place. She didn't have the time. The Forget Me Not Boutique required every spare minute. She decided on that disappointing drive home to focus on her business and save dating for a day when she didn't have to worry about how she was going to pay her employees. She needed to stick by that resolve now more than ever.

It worked well, aside from Mom's unwanted matchmaking.

But with Brayden, it was better this way, them staying friends.

"Sarra. Where does she live?"

"Phoenix."

"Married? Kids?"

Brayden took a step back and assessed the top branches, wearing a frown that suggested he was not satisfied with the shape. "You ask a lot of questions."

"You answer a lot of them with short, punctuated answers that create more questions."

From behind the cover of the thick tree, she couldn't see his expression. Only the tips of his fingers back at work on the branches. "I don't have any nieces or nephews, if that's what you want to know. No additional names to memorize."

The mystery of Brayden's sister continued. At least she got a name this time. She gave up on learning more about the elusive Sarra and moved on. "Grandparents?"

"Down to one. Grandma on my dad's side." Elsie's sleepy growl filled the silence as Ava waited not so patiently for him to continue. In all fairness, this was the most Brayden had opened up since those first few weeks as neighbors. When she decided a rescheduled date wasn't in their future, he clammed up. They'd never regained that early effortless friendship. She missed it. "I lost my grandpa—dad's side—a little over a year ago."

Ava stretched her neck around the tree again, unprepared for the emotion lingering in his dark brown eyes. He'd never mentioned this before. Surprising, with it so recent. It had to be a clue as to why he really moved to Sunset Ridge. "You two were close."

"At one time." Brayden met her gaze for a mere second, and something unusual happened. Ava's stomach fluttered as if a butterfly had been trapped inside. "He taught me how to work with wood. Everything I know about making bookshelves and coffee tables with careful skill. He's the whole reason I wanted to live here, where there was a wood-working shop already set up. It makes me feel closer to him somehow."

"I'm sorry for your loss."

"That's life, right? Over in a blink of an eye if you're not careful."

Something important had been left unsaid, and Ava desperately wanted to know what it was. She felt as if it were the key to everything where Brayden Young was concerned. She chose her next question carefully, uncertain he would answer at all. "Why did you move to Sunset Ridge? It's kind of off the beaten trail."

Brayden stepped back from the tree in search of his fountain drink, but a single loud slurp rendered the cup empty of everything but ice. "Long story," he said evasively. "I don't know about your side of the tree, but mine is ready for lights."

She came around to the front, shocked how perfect the branches he'd worked were shaped and fluffed. It was better than the floor model. "How did you do that so fast?"

"I'm that good."

"Well, if you're such a tree genius, why don't you finish my side while I test the lights."

"On it."

Elsie let out a groan and stretched on her side from the dog bed Brayden had placed in front of the couch. She'd been happily napping ever since the halibut tacos disappeared. Her eyes fluttered open for a split second, then fell shut again. Ava envied the pup's easy life, and naps whenever she craved them. Ava hadn't taken a nap in at least four years. Maybe longer.

She settled onto the end of the couch near an outlet and set to work plugging in strand after strand, disappointed at the number of old strands that wouldn't light at all. *Glad we stocked up on new ones.*

Her mind raced, wondering if Brayden was only opening up because he had no other choice. Whatever he kept from her his mom might reveal. It only stirred more questions. Ava didn't care to feel so unsettled about it all. Secrets had never done anyone she knew any good. Kinley suffered for years not knowing her father's true identity because someone was so set on keeping it a secret. And Laurel, she kept a secret from Ava when she boarded a plane with Chase and eloped. And again, six months later when they broke up the marriage and she left without saying goodbye.

Ava despised secrets.

"Tell me more about your gift baskets," Brayden said, shaping branches at an alarming speed, as if he'd done this many times before. "I didn't see any in the store last time I stopped in."

"You hardly leave this property," Ava countered, slipping her phone from her pocket and adding a couple of notes about the store display she planned to put together tomorrow. She still had to track down boxes and assemble three dozen baskets. *Guess I'll sleep after Christmas is over.*

"I went out twice just today."

"I should mark that down on my calendar." She tossed another dead strand in a pile and went for the next. She used to have enough lights to suffocate a massive tree, line the ceilings, and light up the front of her house. At this rate, they'd have to go back to the hardware store to get more. "I thought the baskets might be a way to showcase what the Forget Me Not has to offer. They're filled with Alaskan-made goodies, just like the store."

"I think they're a great idea," Brayden said. "But aren't you selling them a little late in the season? Christmas is next week."

"Yeah." Ava let out a heavy sigh, wishing she'd brought her soda with her to the couch. No way she was getting so close to Brayden with those unpredictable butterflies clouding her judgment. "I just got the ribbon in this morning." She didn't want to admit that she'd had to purchase as much as possible on clearance. She bargained with her wholesalers, too. Every penny had to count. "I'm hoping to mostly sell them around town. Maybe see if I can get a couple of gift shops in Seward to sell them on consignment." Except she had no clue when she'd find the time to make it to any other small towns with Mom inbound.

"Suppose shipping them to the lower forty-eight is out," Brayden murmured.

"They'd never make it on time. Perks of living in Alaska." Ava abandoned her soda and went for a bottled water from her fridge instead. "I'm half tempted to drop the cards in mailboxes around town. Not sure the postmaster would appreciate that."

It was the mixed-up expression on Brayden's face that gave her pause—the one that morphed between sour, contemplative, and cautious.

"Out with it."

"Those cards. They're a great idea."

"But?"

"Let me design some new templates. You don't have to use them, but I think you might like what I come up with."

Ava lifted an eyebrow, the mystery of Brayden's past pulling at her curiosity even more. He didn't even have a website for his woodworking, yet he was suddenly a graphic designer? "What's wrong with my cards?"

"You didn't list your website, for one."

Shoot. He was right. Which only reminded Ava that she needed to add the baskets to her website inventory tonight. Tomorrow she needed to put flyers up in the local businesses, assemble as many as possible, and set up an impossible-to-miss display at the store. "I'll add that."

"Are you *that* opposed to taking a chance on me?"

Heat crept up her neck and she turned away. *He's talking about the flyers, right?* "Are you trying to tell me that you—the woodworker—have a hidden talent for graphic design?" She was used to doing most things on her own. Splurging on fancy marketing graphics was a thing of the past. She wasn't terrible at it, but someone else might be better. That much she could admit. She'd taught herself how because it was the best for the bottom line.

Brayden stepped back from the tree. "Send me the template," he dared, not looking at her as he fixed a stray branch. "I'll send you some mockups. What's the worst I could do? If you don't like them, don't use them."

"I can't pay you."

"I didn't ask you to."

"Why do you want to help me?"

When Brayden turned his gaze on her, that butterfly fluttered to life again. Heck, it might've invited a partner to play. "It's Christmas. My grandpa was big on helping people. Especially at Christmas."

"Wow."

"What?"

"You answered a question without being super mysterious."

Brayden let out a laugh as he moved into the kitchen to clean up the dinner mess. "What about Anchorage?"

Ava set down the last strand in its own pile—it was the only one that fully worked—and pushed off the couch. Elsie's eyes blinked open, likely at the crinkling of wrappers. She pushed out of her dog bed, missing on the first attempt. "All the craft fairs are booked solid. I'm on half a dozen waitlists, but I'm so far down on the list I can't even hope to make one." If only her idea had struck her sooner, maybe she could've planned better. "Planning is usually one of my strengths—and still one if my mom asks—but this year has been a little . . . hectic."

"I bet you're more on top of this than you give yourself credit for," Brayden said. "But a little collaborative effort never hurt anything. Maybe I can help. We'll be spending more time together than we expected, right? If we don't, our cover will be busted. How many of these baskets do you have, anyway?"

Ava let out a laugh. "You'd never believe me without seeing it for yourself."

Stepping out from the kitchen and waving a hand toward the stairs, he said, "Lead the way."

"Right now?"

"I thought you had everything in your garage."

"I do."

"Then amaze me."

He followed much too closely for Ava's sanity. It was that dang flutter again. Her guard was dropping, and it didn't seem she was capable of stopping it.

It was a *fake* relationship. Nothing more. Sure, when she first met her neighbor, she had it bad for him. Brayden Young was attractive and mysterious. Every available woman in Sunset Ridge had their interest piqued at his arrival in town. But he stood her up and blamed it on falling asleep. The excuse still bothered her.

"There's not much room," she said, hand on the doorknob to the garage.

"I'll manage."

Ava pulled the door open and flipped the light switch, stepping to the side. The dim overhead light washed over dozens of shelves stacked as high as her garage could accommodate. Each was packed with baskets, cellophane, holiday-themed crinkle paper, and all the goodies for each basket in bulk. She didn't have room for the ribbon, and kept it in a cluttered spare bedroom.

"Wow. This is quite the setup." Brayden wandered into the garage, following the only tight path he could. He studied every shelf with such rapt interest that Ava felt flattered.

"It's too much," she said. "No way I can sell *all* of these before Christmas." Never mind that she needed to sell ninety percent to sleep well on Christmas Eve. "It was cheaper to buy everything in bulk quantities." She followed a few steps behind him, picking up an ornament and setting it back down. "Plus, I can customize the baskets with this much inventory. No two will be identical."

When Brayden didn't say anything, she yearned to ask him about the notice. Maybe it would be easier to rip off the Band-Aid. Easier for him to know the truth and why it was so imperative that she keep her mom as far away from the store as possible. She wanted to trust him. But the words wouldn't form.

"I still need to find some boxes I can hide under red sheets for my store display," she said, feeling as though she had to say *something*.

Brayden turned at a corner, and she nearly collided into him. "I have wooden boxes in my shop."

She grabbed a shelf pole, causing the wooden stirring spoons with moose and bears carved into them to rattle. "How many?"

Steadying the shelf with his strong grip, the spoons quieted. "More than enough for a display. And I might even have an idea about these baskets."

"What idea?"

Brayden flashed her a smirk that she usually found annoying, but this time made her pulse double. *That's not good.* "I'll let you know soon."

Ava let out an incredulous laugh, realizing how close they stood together. She should take a step back, but she couldn't get her feet to do anything but remain firmly planted in place. "And there you go right back to being mysterious."

"It's my best quality."

"I don't know about *best*, but definitely most prominent."

When Brayden reached out a hand toward her cheek, Ava stopped breathing. Was he really going to kiss her? Right here in her dimly lit garage? His finger hooked a strand of hair stuck to her temple and tucked it behind her ear. "I think we're going to do just fine."

"What?" The question came out as a raspy whisper.

He dropped his hand and moved forward. "With our mothers. They'll never suspect a thing."

Chapter Six

Brayden

The next morning, Brayden arrived with two large coffees in hand. He forgot he'd gone through the specialty brew he purchased at the Forget Me Not and was forced to give Black Bear Coffee his business since her store wasn't open yet. He was back to working nights in the woodshed to keep up with orders. At this rate, the local coffee shop would be set for the next year.

He let out a yawn so obnoxious it caused Elsie to bark outside Ava's front door. Before he could hit the doorbell with his elbow, the door popped open.

"Oh, good, you have coffee! I just emptied the

pot." Her eyes sparkled as she took the cup and a sip. "Come in, sorry. I don't operate well without caffeine. Maybe something else to note for the whole mom invasion. I love coffee more than any sane person should."

Brayden already knew that about Ava, but most did. He shrugged out of his coat as Elsie trotted up the split staircase behind Ava. He stole an extra moment out of sight to fight another yawn. He'd lied when he told her he was caught up on orders. Though everything in the woodshed wasn't promised until after the new year, he couldn't be certain he'd still be in town. He needed to finish and deliver them all by Christmas Eve to be safe.

"Did you get the mockups I sent you?" he asked, kicking off his boots and slogging up the stairs. He'd been up until after two last night creating marketing cards, brushing off rusty skills, and agonizing over getting the designs just perfect. He had a plan for those cards, and they had to wow not only Ava, but a former client of his as well for his idea to work.

"Saw the email. Haven't had a chance to open it." Ava bustled around her small kitchen, but it wasn't until he saw what she was cooking on the stove that he placed the aroma. "Hope you like Western omelets."

"I do." Brayden caught himself lost in a moment where all this might be normal. Mornings together where he brought the coffee and Ava made them breakfast. Or the other way around. He wasn't picky. But the reality, whether or not he wanted to face it, was that he might very well be in Austin soon. Sunset Ridge and mornings with Ava might be but a distant memory.

"Sit down." She pointed with an elbow to the table. She'd cleared just enough of the Christmas decorations for the two of them to squeeze in plates.

Elsie's head swiveled between the kitchen and the living room window. The window won out. She plopped down and stared outside. Brayden had never met a dog more content to window watch than this one. He wondered if she'd like Texas or resent him for taking her away from the snow and his treat-generous neighbor.

Brayden wanted to tell his mom no, but it wasn't that simple.

"Need help?" he asked.

"Nope." She whisked out of the kitchen, dropping one plate in front of him, then set another at her catty-corner spot. She grabbed her laptop and made room by pushing the pile of stuffed snowmen as far as they would go. One dropped off. Once she made enough space for the laptop, she recovered the fallen snowman before Elsie could get any ideas about a new toy. "I'm curious what you came up with."

Brayden cut into his omelet with a fork to hide nerves he shouldn't feel. He didn't get this jittery around multi-million-dollar clients. But Ava's approval felt like the most important pitch of his life. "I sent a few different options. They'll look best printed on glossy cardstock, but it's not necessary."

Fork clattering against the plate, Ava lost sight of her breakfast and became enamored with her screen. "Brayden, these are . . . holy jingle bells!" She spun the laptop toward him as if he hadn't seen his own work. "These are ten times better than mine. Maybe a hundred."

Her praise warmed his heart in way it hadn't been warmed in years. "Glad you like them."

"You might've just saved Christmas." Her eyes doubled in size and she pushed the laptop closed. "I didn't mean that. I just meant—"

Brayden placed his hand on top of hers and braced for her rejection. But when two seconds passed, then three, and she didn't shimmy away, he decided now was the moment to be brave. Even if she hated him for it. "I know, Ava."

She stared at their joined hands. "What are you

talking about?" But her question came out weak and quiet.

"I didn't *mean* to read the letter, but I did."

As expected, Ava yanked her hand away and stomped off toward the kitchen with her still-full plate. "You tell me that *now*?" she snapped over the breakfast bar. She wanted to be mad, that much he could tell, but her usual fire wasn't as strong.

"You've suspected it all along."

"And still you pretended like you never saw the notice."

"I didn't want to embarrass you, not in front of Kinley." But the truth was more complicated than that. He and Ava might not have been as close as he wanted, but he was good at reading people. Figuring them out. It was the quality that helped him please their toughest marketing clients. Had he admitted the truth that day, Ava's pride would've suffered immensely. The Christmas basket idea might never have been born. "I haven't told anyone."

"And that makes it better?" Tears dotted the corners of her eyes and Brayden pushed out of his seat.

He posted himself in the narrow walkway into the kitchen, giving her space if she wanted it, but offering comfort if she preferred that instead. It was a dangerous tango they were playing at. He couldn't allow himself to get close to her. Not when he might uproot his entire cozy life in days. Yet he couldn't seem to stay away.

"No, it doesn't make it better."

She swiped hastily at a tear.

Bravely, Brayden took a step into the kitchen, then two. He reached out both hands and rested them on her arms. "I want to help you turn this around," he said gently, unsettled by the electricity that hummed in the air between them. "I can help. Please let me."

"It's not your problem."

"Kind of is now."

Ava let out an exasperated laugh. "Do explain that one."

"Your mom." He shuffled forward an inch, and tipped her chin up with his knuckle. "You don't want her to know how serious this situation has gotten. I'm willing to bet no one else knows. Not even your best friend. But like it or not, we're Facebook official to this town. Your burdens are mine now, especially while your mom is around, and I won't let you face her alone. That's not what a fake boyfriend would do."

"What would a fake boyfriend do?" she asked,

her words hardly a whisper. The space between them seemed to evaporate. Brayden needed to turn around and run before something happened he couldn't take back. If he had to leave for Texas, he wanted to part friends. Not with Ava hating him for leading her on.

So why weren't his feet shuffling backward or his hands dropping?

A shrill ring accompanied with a bark from Elsie severed the intense moment. Brayden released an audible sigh of relief as Ava pushed around him and lunged for her phone on the table. He'd never dated anyone else in Sunset Ridge, and now he remembered why. "Your mom?" he guessed, hiding his face behind the kitchen pillar.

"Kinley." Ava's tone held apology. "I'll just be a minute."

He nodded as Ava disappeared down the hall and closed her bedroom door, clearing his plate from the table and joining Elsie at the window. His breathing was still heavy and unpredictable. He'd almost *kissed* her. He could laugh off a lot of things, but that one would be hard. A kiss could change everything. Until he figured out what to do about Mom retiring ahead of schedule, he couldn't let feelings get in the way. He didn't want to hurt Ava. Or himself.

Elsie leaned against his leg, demanding head scratches. "What a mess, huh, girl?"

Brayden liked Ava. That had never changed.

But his mom's insistence that he had an obligation to take over the *family* company and needed to be home to learn how had grown stronger and more insistent each week he stayed in Sunset Ridge without plans of moving home. Tomorrow she'd no doubt drop the bomb that she moved up her retirement date and backed him into a corner.

He'd once enjoyed the fast-paced life. The thrill, the rush, the constant demand. Even hiding out in Sunset Ridge, he had to admit there were days he missed it. Working on Ava's flyers late last night reminded him as much. But Brayden had changed a lot over the last several months. He wasn't the same person anymore. It wasn't only the accident that changed him, but Sunset Ridge.

"Sorry about that," Ava apologized. "I'm Kinley's maid of honor. Her wedding isn't until June, but she's turned into quite the planner."

"This town has a lot of weddings," he said with a chuckle.

"Weddings!" Ava's eyes doubled in size—they

did that a lot lately, but he found it adorable. "You'll have to be my plus-one."

"For a wedding in June?" *Might not even be here.* "Are we expecting another ambush this summer?" He meant it as a joke, but Ava's anxious expression didn't morph into amused.

"Cadence and Ford. Their wedding is two days before Christmas. I don't know about your mom, but mine won't leave until after the holidays are over. I'm just hoping she doesn't stay until New Year's. Do you have a suit?"

"Yes."

"Really?"

"Really." He had a closet full of them but no excuse to wear one. He didn't expect to need one in Alaska, but Mom taught him to always be prepared. He hadn't been able to break *all* of his old habits. "I'll be your plus-one, don't worry."

"How are you so calm about everything?" A smile finally graced her lips. "It's completely unfair."

"A little yin and yang is probably why we make such a perfect couple," he added in jest. "Makes everything more convincing."

"Keep reminding yourself you said that when my mom tries to name our future children," Ava mumbled. "Look, I have to meet Kinley for lunch to talk bridesmaid dresses. Kind of the last thing I care about right now, but I promised her days ago. We need to get these baskets together stat."

"You sound thrilled," Brayden teased.

"Picking out fancy dresses isn't really my cup of tea." Ava dug her clipboard out from beneath a pile of stuffed snowmen on the table. "That was always more Laurel's thing." She said the last in a mutter.

"Who's Laurel?"

All hints of a smile vanished. "Someone who used to be a friend. Not important. Anyway, I have to break at noon. If you're planning to stick around and help, we're going into overachiever mode."

"Sign me up."

He helped Ava clear out the empty holiday boxes, then bring up dozens of baskets and cut off the clearance tags. He had to give her credit. She was frugal in her big plan without sacrificing quality. Smart in more ways than one. And since no two baskets were identical, each one would feel unique. Maybe Mom would see that she was special after all. She always did appreciate a smart businesswoman. "What next?"

"Here." She slid him a printed spreadsheet, stapled five pages deep. He flipped through the packet, impressed by her level of detail for such a spontaneous design. Every item on her labeled shelves was entered into a category. Each basket had a set number of each category. Her random baskets had quite the system. "This is insanely organized. You weren't kidding."

"You sound surprised."

"I shouldn't be," he answered honestly. "But I've seen your office."

Ava tossed a puffy snowman at him from across the room. "I'll have you know I cleaned that up yesterday."

"By shoving everything you didn't need in a box and sticking it under your desk?" he speculated.

"Have you been spying on me?"

Brayden laughed. "Lucky guess."

With Christmas music playing in the background and the coffee pot brewing, they set to work assembling the first three dozen baskets for Ava's store display. He'd offered to lend her wooden boxes to help set it all up, and spent an hour last night constructing a few with scrap lumber.

"Wow," Ava said when they finished the last one. "I haven't climbed that many steps in ages. I'm going to be sore tomorrow." She laughed.

"It's almost noon. You should go."

Ava scanned the room, appearing overwhelmed

for the first time since that morning in the kitchen. They hadn't spoken again about the letter, and he wasn't going to push it now. He admitted the truth. The rest, well, it would wait. Elsie yawned near the window, poking her head up behind a round basket wrapped in gold cellophane. "I need to get these to the store." She let out a defeated sigh. "I'm the worst maid of honor in history."

"Go," Brayden said, taking the phone from Ava's hands before she could successfully text her friend and cancel. "I'll load it all up in my truck and take it to the store for you."

"But—"

"We're a team, right?"

Ava looked up at him, and it reminded him how badly he'd wanted to kiss her earlier. How badly he *still* wanted to kiss her. He only wished he could blame it on mistletoe or something equally cliché. "You're walking into an ambush, you know. Glenda and Becca will probably pepper you with questions."

"I know."

When Ava hesitated at the top of the stairs, he felt the earlier tension return. "Why are you really doing all this?" Ava asked, folding her arms over her soft green sweater. Her gentle expression turned serious as she studied him uncomfortably close.

"Don't get me wrong, I really appreciate the help, but this isn't your problem, mom dilemma or not."

Brayden gulped a swallow, unsure how to answer her question without revealing how far he'd gone out of his way. "It keeps me busy," he said, instantly regretting the word choice at Ava's cringe.

"Maybe one of these days, you'll tell me what you've been running from." Ava hurried down the stairs and shimmied into her coat. "Or maybe your mom will."

"Don't count on it."

"I know this is fake and all, but I'm not a quitter. Your mom will *love* me before she leaves."

"That a challenge?"

"I have a few days to win her over." She winked. "Just wait and see."

"Good luck." Brayden doubted his mom would stay in Sunset Ridge a single day longer than she deemed necessary. She'd never miss her fancy office holiday party, not with such an important announcement to make. And in between, she'd work nonstop from the lodge. The questionable cell service alone might drive Mom out of Sunset Ridge within hours.

Ava rushed out the door, leaving him to load up the baskets.

Once finished, he was faced with an expectant dog.

"Sorry, Elsie. You'll have to sit this one out. No room in that truck right now, and Ava would kill us both if you put a paw through one of her baskets." Brayden knelt down and squeezed the golden against him. She groaned and squirmed, but ultimately licked him on the cheek. "We'll go for a long ride this afternoon, promise. We have a special delivery to make."

He locked up both places and headed to the Forget Me Not Boutique, prepared for the ambush wearing a smile.

Chapter Seven

Ava

"Isn't this beautiful?" Kinley let out a heavy sigh that frosted the wintery air and momentarily blocked the mountain view she praised.

"It's the perfect spot," Ava agreed, shoving her gloveless hands in her coat pockets. When she agreed to meet Kinley for lunch to discuss bridesmaid dresses, she thought they'd be at Willamina's Big Dipper, in a corner booth, enjoying a hearty bowl of soup. She rushed out of the house too quickly to remember gloves. At least she had her festive scarf. "I'm glad it'll be warmer in June."

"I have to run it by Ryder still. He wanted to get married on a boat."

Ava sputtered a laugh. "Why am I not surprised?"

"We compromised on the outdoor concept. I'll have to bring him up here later, but I needed a second opinion. It'll be a small ceremony, so we don't need much space for chairs and all that." The way Kinley's eyes sparkled with excitement was the exact reason Ava had never shared her secret burden with her best friend. It wasn't that she worried Kinley would judge her ability to run a successful business. It was that she never felt right spoiling her friend's happiness with a problem she created herself.

"It's perfect, Kin."

"I hope Tillie approves." Kinley tore her gaze from the mountains and settled on Ava. "Speaking of wonderfully overbearing mothers, when does yours get in?"

"Tomorrow."

"You really think this whole fake relationship thing with Brayden is going to keep her off your back?"

"It'll keep her from setting me up on random dates. She's bad enough from three thousand miles away. Could you imagine how she'd be, let loose *in* town?" Ava bounced from one foot to the other, not wanting to rush Kinley. But her fingertips were frozen, and her toes were following suit.

"Poor Pete."

"Not poor Pete. Poor Ava. You know how that would've ended." Ava shook her head, memories of past dates set up by Mom going south floating around in her mind. She couldn't say no to the setups without being the bad guy, but she always ended up being the one to let *him* down anyway. "He'd be nice but strange. Not my type. But at the end of the date, I'd have to dodge a kiss and break his heart."

"Have you even met him?"

"Does it matter?"

"Maybe." Kinley took one last lingering look at the mountain view then spun around. "Sure it has nothing to do with a certain fake boyfriend who might not be so fake at all?"

The memory of Brayden in the kitchen this morning, saving her from her own tears and a complete meltdown as he nearly kissed her—a second time—weakened her defenses. The topic was too dangerous. Ava didn't trust her own words. She cleared her throat. "It's fake, Kinley."

"It would be okay if it wasn't."

"Don't go there."

"You never gave him a second chance. Maybe you should. A *real* one, not a fake one. See if it goes anywhere. If you insist on waiting until after your mothers both leave town, then fine. But think about it, Ava, please. You deserve someone, too."

"We good here? I'm frozen like a popsicle." Ava bounced heavier on her feet to emphasize her point and hopefully steer the conversation away from Brayden. She couldn't think about any of that right now. She had a display to set up in her store, flyers to print, and businesses to visit. Until her store was saved from foreclosure, she couldn't think about anything else. The butterflies would have to stand down. "I really need to get back to the store."

"Yes, we're done. Thank you for coming out here with me even though it's twelve degrees."

"Nine."

Kinley looked over her shoulder at the view one last time, such happiness in those eyes when she turned them back to Ava. "I can't believe I'm getting *married*. To Ryder Grant, of all people."

Ava looped her arm through Kinley's and pulled them down the snow-packed path. The sooner they got to her car, the sooner her fingers could thaw. Heat. She craved heat. "You two are perfect for each other," Ava said, and meant it. "It was pretty cool that you were in the Army and all, but I'm so glad you live here now."

"Almost like the old trio is back together again, huh?"

Biting down on her lip, Ava focused on the path beneath her feet. She wasn't ready to talk about Laurel. She might not ever be ready to discuss the best friend who went behind her back in such a big way. "Do you have to work this afternoon?"

"You'll have to see her, Ava. She's a bridesmaid."

"I could use some help with flyers if you're free."

"Ava."

"I'm not ready to think about that yet. She married my brother in secret, then dumped him." Ava sucked in a breath and squeezed her eyes shut. Her life was chaotic enough without bringing Laurel into the mix. With any luck, she wouldn't have to see her until the actual wedding. Her former best friend couldn't even be bothered to set aside her crazy life to make it to Kinley's engagement party, and those two spoke all the time. "Can we just—" When Kinley yanked to her to a halt, she nearly tumbled forward. "What the jingle bells, Kin!"

"Moose."

"What?"

Kinley kept them shuffling backward as Ava

regained her footing and her gaze landed on Ed. Standing in the middle of the path between them and the car, chewing on a branch. His ears perked when their eyes locked. She wondered if he remembered their encounter yesterday morning. Did moose have sharp memories? She'd have to look it up.

"I'm too cold for this," Ava said, teeth starting to chatter. Most December days the temperature stayed in the double digits in Sunset Ridge. But a cold spell had hit overnight and dropped their tolerable thirty to single digits. "Ed, why are you determined to make me late everywhere I go?"

The moose turned his massive body in the path, pointing at them. He tilted his head, almost as if he were trying to understand the question. But Ava knew it was ridiculous. Ed was many things, but he wasn't some magical being who could understand English.

"It's your scarf," Kinley said.

Looking down at the holiday scarf she'd purchased from her own store, she groaned. The red balls *did* look a little like berries. "I really like this scarf," she said, unwrapping it. "But I'm too cold for this crap." She wadded it up and tossed it on the ground between them and the moose, hoping Ed would take her peace offering and let them go.

The bull moose snorted hard enough to form a cloud.

"I don't think it worked," Kinley said. "Any other tricks up your sleeve?"

Ava tightened her grip on Kinley's arm. The path led only to the landing where Kinley planned to marry Ryder. There was nowhere to run, unless they were prepared to jump over a steep, rocky cliff. "Ed doesn't even *like* me."

"Maybe I should call Ryder." Kinley's words stuttered with her shivering. Ed took a deliberate step forward, stared at Ava, then dropped his attention to the scarf. "Wait, maybe he's taking the bait."

"Don't hold your breath," Ava muttered. She had three dozen baskets to arrange, and right now, she felt certain they were piled up in a corner *not* selling themselves. Why couldn't she have an epic Ed story like everyone else in town? But no, Ed had never saved her from a black bear or appeared at her kitchen window in search of blueberry handouts. "He'll be extra irritable when he realizes he's been duped again."

"There's something you should know about Laurel—"

"Nope. Not doing this now," Ava snapped.

"Ava—"

"Finally, he's going." Scarf in mouth, Ed turned and trotted into the woods with agonizing slowness. "I really liked that scarf."

"I'll buy you another," Kinley offered. "Let's go. I'm frozen."

The heater in Ava's sedan waited until the last block to the Forget Me Not to kick out warm air. Hardly enough to thaw her frigid fingers. She blamed Ed for scrambling her brain and causing her to forget about her auto start. She yearned to wrap her hands around a steaming cup of coffee from Black Bear. But such frivolities were less and less in the budget until she turned things around. She'd save her next coffee splurge for after she sold her first hundred baskets.

"Is that Brayden's truck?" Kinley pointed down the street at the blue quad cab driving away from the Forget Me Not.

"Yeah. He dropped off the gift baskets and some boxes for the display."

"Fake, huh?"

"He's *helping*. That's all. He brought some baskets because it would've taken me five trips in my car."

"Sure, okay."

Ava parked her car. She'd been with Kinley

nearly two hours. She couldn't imagine it took that long to unload everything. Unless he had to make two trips. Or if something was damaged. *Please let nothing be broken.* In order to make that balloon payment next week, she needed every basket sale she could get. She couldn't afford to lose a single one to human error. "You don't have to stick around if you're busy. After I get this display together, I have to print flyers and pester every business in town."

"The baskets sound like a little bit of a big deal," Kinley said, holding the door open for Ava.

"Just last minute," Ava admitted. "God Rest Ye Merry Gentlemen" floated faintly out the door. Ava wished she could play Christmas music in her shop all year long, but she wouldn't torture anyone else with her guilty pleasure. "I didn't get all the supplies in until yesterday. So now I have a whole lot of inventory and only a few days to sell them."

"You could probably put the leftovers on clearance *after* Christmas," Kinley said, pulling the door closed behind her. The bells clamored harder with the gust of wind, saving Ava from explaining she might not have that luxury this year.

"Maybe."

Ava braced for the chaos inside the door, but she was met with soft Christmas music and laughter.

Maybe even clapping, though with Glenda it was hard to tell. She clapped at everything. "Ava, look!" Glenda waved her over to the corner she'd cleared for the display.

"I'll say it again," Kinley said. "Fake, huh?"

Where she expected a pile of boxes and baskets to cover the floor, a beautifully crafted display was in its place. She wasn't sure how he managed it, but Brayden worked fast. The wooden boxes he promised were stacked in diagonal patterns that offered multiple shelves and levels for her assortment. The red tablecloths she'd set aside draped over the boxes. Every landing held two or three baskets. The various colored cellophane wrapping was sprinkled throughout, like Christmas lights on a tree.

"Glenda, did you and Becca—"

"Oh, no!" Glenda's enormous smile had to hurt her cheeks. "Brayden did all this. I was swamped with customers while he was here. Couldn't even help him unload anything. Isn't it wonderful? We've already sold four of them!"

Ava walked a full circle around the display, astonished that Brayden's quick work looked so much better than the display she had envisioned in her mind. "Man of many hidden talents," she murmured under her breath, impressed.

"You should bring him dinner tonight when you get home," Kinley suggested. "Food's better than a simple thank you."

"Oh, Brayden won't be home tonight," Glenda said, the surprise of her declaration too quick for Ava to mask her disappointment from Kinley. She'd never hear the end of this. "He had to make a delivery in Girdwood. Said to tell you he won't be back until late."

"We could catch him now," Kinley said. "Before he leaves town."

Ava shook her head, the gesture warring with her internal yearning to do as Kinley said. But one kindness didn't change anything. Brayden said it himself, he had the time to help. Nothing more. "I'll see him tomorrow. Thank him with donuts or something. I need to print off flyers."

"Donuts?" Kinley questioned. "This is worth more than donuts, don't you think?"

"The flyers are on your desk," Glenda said, saving Ava an embarrassing explanation.

"But I haven't printed them yet." Before Glenda could say it, Ava cut in, "Brayden?"

Glenda nodded as eagerly as her smile was bright. "You've really snagged a good one, Ava. Make sure you invite me to your wedding."

Kinley shoved Ava into her office before she could do something foolish, like tell Glenda this was all a big joke. Mom would hover in the store half her visit. It was better that Glenda believe her relationship with Brayden was real. She only hoped her faithful employee and Mom didn't start planning an imaginary wedding together.

A stack of glossy cards sat in the center of Ava's still-cleared desk. She hadn't had time to unpack the contents she'd shoved haphazardly into a box yesterday. She added that to her mental to-do list before Mom arrived.

"Wow, these are stunning!" Kinley turned a card in her hand, the gloss catching in the light. "Did you make these?"

How Ava wished she could take credit for them, if only to keep Kinley from jumping to more conclusions than she already had. "No, I hired them out." Ava picked one up herself, studying the beautiful holiday design that showcased three different size baskets, her website, and her store logo. If only she had these cards weeks ago, she could've collected orders while she waited for the contents to arrive.

"You have to tell me who you used. Might have them make my save the dates."

Ava evaded the question. "Ready to drop these

off with me? I still have to show Rilee how to fill online orders when she gets in and reorganize my office so Mom can't use my messiness against me." After all that was done, she'd be assembling more baskets. Three dozen was only a humble start.

"I just thawed my toes."

"How about I treat us to coffee," Ava offered, feeling generous with a few baskets already sold. "Then we descend on the town?"

Kinley scooped a handful of cards and set them in her purse. "I knew there was a reason I picked you to be my maid of honor. You never overlook the important details."

Chapter Eight

Brayden

Brayden woke to Elsie licking him on the cheek. His back felt stiff and his fingers ached. A chill filled the air. He pushed himself up, discovering he'd fallen asleep on his cot. The woodstove held embers and nothing more. "Did it again, Elsie." He rubbed the dog on the back of her head as a yawn assaulted him.

Last night, Brayden hadn't returned to Sunset Ridge until after ten. He was tired after the drive to and from Anchorage, with a delivery beforehand in Girdwood. He could blame the coffee table, but that stop had been a quick one. A simple drop-off in exchange for a check. It was the errand he ran *after* Girdwood that detained him.

"Let's get inside," he said with a drawn-out yawn. "I need coffee."

He hoped his extra effort and sacrificed sleep resulted in several gift basket sales for the Forget Me Not. With any luck, Ava'd never know he had part in it.

Elsie ran slow circles around him in the snow, investigating fallen branches and odd piles of snow as they made their way through the backyard and up the snow-covered deck stairs. The flurries had flown his whole drive home last night. Shoveling today would wake him up.

Inside, he opened his cupboards in search of coffee, only to remember that he'd emptied the last bag. "Should I get more now?" he asked the dog who was lapping up water. He could stop by Ava's store and pick up a few more bags of Alaskan-brewed coffee. But truth be told, he wasn't ready to see her. Not yet.

The drive had done wonders to his racing thoughts, but hadn't made anything clear. He had responsibilities to his family. A predestined future all mapped out for him. Others relied on him to keep the Young-founded business in the family. Mom would remind him as much when she arrived. That pressure only solidified one thing for him; he didn't want to leave Sunset Ridge. Now or in the future. This was home.

Brayden shoveled both staircases, waking up his sore muscles. He rarely slept out in the woodworking shed anymore, and he hadn't intended to do it last night. The cot he stored out there was from his early days in town when his schedule was upside down and sleeping normal hours was out of the question. The accident had haunted him a lot more then.

He'd been pushing too hard. A moment's rest nearly cost him the whole morning. He'd fallen asleep and missed Ava leaving for the store. Missed his chance to warn her about the text from Mom late last night that demanded dinner at the lodge at four.

Her text message invite didn't include Ava, but he was bringing her anyway. It was supposedly the whole reason she was coming to Alaska, but he couldn't pretend to know without outing his sister for tipping him off.

Time. He needed more time.

"Want to go for a ride?" he asked Elsie.

The golden wagged her tail eagerly and raced down the split staircase to the front door. He chuckled, meeting her there. One look in the entryway mirror, though, and Brayden turned back. "Sorry, girl. Give me two minutes."

He splashed water on his face, but it did little to hide one stubborn cot-created crease. At least it helped with his wild hair and otherwise smashed-up beard. Elsie barked her impatience from the hallway. Car rides brought out her inner puppy. She'd apparently slept off the excitement of yesterday's trek and was eager for more. "I'm coming, girl."

He led them to the garage and helped Elsie into the truck. Though she could still jump in, it was always accompanied with moans and groans. Arthritis and stiff joints of an aging dog, no doubt. Brayden couldn't bear to hear her grunt in pain when he had the power to make things more comfortable for her.

Another yawn assaulted him as he reached the edge of the driveway. This one made his eyes water. If time was on his side, he would've crawled straight into bed last night. But it wasn't.

What would he tell Mom?

For years, he accepted that he would run Young Elite Marketing Services. He embraced it, and looked forward to the challenge. It meant less personal client work and more overseeing everyone else. Making the big decisions from the top instead of feeling the impact of them personally. But it was the next step on a ladder he'd climbed so high on. Never had he considered an alternative future.

Until his truck slid off the road and tumbled down a steep, rocky ditch and landed upside down in a creek that he later learned was normally five feet deep. A drought was the reason he didn't drown. The accident should've killed him, in more ways than one.

But it didn't.

He was a changed man.

"I don't know, girl." Elsie, eyes forward and alert, wagged her tail. "This isn't supposed to be so hard. It was always my path, but I don't want it anymore." But with Sarra accepting another job with the company's major competitor, he didn't want the company Dad founded to be sold outside the family. It didn't feel right. Running it himself and leaving Alaska behind didn't either. "What do I do, huh?"

He parked his truck outside the coffee shop, opting to go inside instead of through the backed-up drive-thru line. Maybe he'd bring Harold a cup along with his supplies list for his next project. He didn't mind Elsie in the store once in a while, and the two were overdue for a chat.

"Back again so soon?" Charlene, the owner of

Black Bear, greeted him, her smile welcoming. "You better be careful. You just might become a regular."

"Not my fault you make some pretty amazing coffee." Another yawn tried to escape, but he stifled this one.

"What would you like?"

Brayden studied the menu and chose a couple of lattes with peppermint accents. Harold pretended to drink his coffee black, but he never snubbed a coffee with a little added flavor as long as there was a lid to hide the whipped cream. It was their secret.

"One for the girlfriend, then?"

Without caffeine already coursing through his veins, Brayden wasn't prepared for the question. He stumbled through an answer. "Uh, no. Not this morning. Maybe later, though." One thing he'd learned about Sunset Ridge was that everyone knew everyone else's business. Or thought they did. It took some getting used to, and made it impossibly hard to remain off the radar. He was thankful he'd been able to keep his wealth under wraps for so long. That no one had found him out, which would've been fairly effortless with a LinkedIn search.

Sunset Ridge was filled with good, trusting people. Their nosiness often meant they genuinely cared.

"You two make a great couple," Charlene said over the plastic partition as he moved down the line and let the woman behind him order. "Didn't think it'd take this long with you two being neighbors and all. Better late than never, you know."

He looked over his shoulder at the truck, hoping to divert the conversation away from topics he couldn't handle without a full cup of coffee consumed. *How late did I work last night?* Elsie's front paws rested on the dashboard as she stared in. "You have any of those dog treats?" he asked, already knowing the answer since he'd asked a barista a couple of weeks ago. "Like the ones they have at the Forget Me Not?"

"No," Charlene answered as she worked. "But you know, that's a great idea. People keep asking. Guess I'll have to call up Ava and get some here to hand out. In the meantime, I can offer a pup cup."

Brayden took the coffees and declined the offer. "Too much sugar and she'll be barking at trees that look at her funny all day long," he said with a wink. "Have a nice day, now." He pushed open the door and nearly took out Ava.

She stumbled backward just in time to keep from being flattened against the salt-covered pavement. "You're awake," she said, stopping in the open doorway. With only a single sip of coffee in him, he couldn't be certain of the twinkle in her eyes. The one that suggested she was happy to see him. Maybe even missed him last night. "I was concerned when Elsie didn't show up for her morning treat."

"Slept in on accident. Still a little groggy, but Elsie woke me up." Realizing the door was wide open and cold air was rushing in, he let it fall closed. Staring at the two cups in hand, guilt overcame him that one wasn't for Ava. "I need some supplies from the hardware store," he explained before she could ask. "Thought I'd butter Harold up with some coffee. Rumor has it this morning's crossword is a doozy."

"Good call." She stuffed her hands into her pockets, gloves no doubt forgotten again. Maybe the desk he was making her was too much. A simple pair of gloves might be the perfect gift for a woman who couldn't seem to remember to bring them anywhere she went.

"Any word from your mom?" he asked, prolonging his news as long as possible. He didn't want to spoil her morning with a stuffy dinner invite a minute sooner than he had to.

"She's doing some shopping in Anchorage this morning. I secretly hope she shops until she drops and decides to stay in a hotel tonight. One more day before battle would be nice." Ava's soft smile drew his gaze to her lips, pulling him in under a spell he was having a harder time breaking. He could fall in love with Ava. He always knew he could, if only he allowed it. But now was the worst time to let that happen.

"I'll keep my fingers crossed."

Ava nodded. "You better get that coffee to Harold before it gets cold."

"Right." Brayden took two steps and stopped. "Ava?"

"Yeah?"

"We have dinner with my mom tonight. At four."

"Dinner at *four*?"

"Well, she's used to the Central Time Zone."

Ava nodded. "Four. Okay. Warren's?"

"Whitmore Patio, inside. I don't think you could pay my mom to eat at Warren's," he added with a laugh. "It's a little *too* small town for her taste. I'll pick you up. We can ride together."

The color drained a bit from Ava's face. "Do I have to wear a cocktail dress or something?"

Brayden glanced at Elsie pacing in the truck, reminding him he only had minutes before Harold locked up and went in search of his own coffee. "No, of course not. I wouldn't ask you to go through all that trouble to impress your fake boyfriend's mom."

"Is that a challenge, Brayden Young?" A smirk formed on those kissable lips, causing his heart to skip a beat then double another. "Just because I don't *like* wearing dresses doesn't mean I won't."

"You're in good spirits," he said, evading. Mom could secretly love Ava, but she'd never admit it on principle. It had been that way for years, for both him and Sarra and anyone they might be dating. Mom found flaws and kept her compliments between pursed lips.

"I sold out of all the baskets you brought over yesterday. Every single one. Can you believe that?"

"That's amazing! Do you have more?"

"Worked on them all last night." She looked down at her ankle boots, shuffling from one foot to another. It was too cold to stand out here like this, but he hated the idea of leaving her behind. It didn't make sense. "Thanks for setting up that display for me, Brayden. You really didn't have to do that."

He shrugged. "I was there. It needed to be done."

"You did a really good job." Ava studied him with too much interest. "*Too* good. But Glenda refuses to take an ounce of credit. Insists it was all you and some Christmas magic up your sleeve."

"You better grab your coffee before the line gets any longer."

Ava pulled open the door again, hesitating as if she might say something important. But all that came out was, "See you at four."

Brayden gave a nod and hurried to his truck. He had hoped that distance yesterday would help him put up a wall. One that was essential for Ava's protection until his mess of a life was sorted out. But despite his best attempts, his feelings were growing stronger, warring with the heavy decision he had to make. If only Mom recognized Sarra's talents before she jumped ship, maybe his sister would be in line to take over the company instead.

His gaze followed Ava through the storefront window until he backed away and headed the short two blocks to the hardware store.

Lights outlined the storefront windows, and one of the trees displayed was filled with ornaments. He clipped Elsie's leash to her collar before lifting her out of the truck, then reached back inside for the coffee.

"Morning, Brayden." Harold accepted the offering with a smile, taking a sip, then giving Elsie head scratches. Brayden didn't miss the flashed smile of approval for the peppermint. "Don't tell my wife I like this stuff." He chortled.

"Wouldn't dream of sharing your secret."

"What do you need today?"

Brayden pulled a list from his pocket. The idea to make Ava a new desk had been born yesterday when he set the flyers in her office. Her desk was old and beaten up. One of the legs wobbled. When he attempted to tighten the loose screw, he noticed the worn hole. Too many attempts to fix the desk over the years had left it worse for wear.

He also spotted the box, filled to the brim with papers, books, and trinkets.

During his drive home last night, he designed her desk in his mind. One with cubbies, slots for notebooks and ledgers, and a better setup for her computer. It was one of the reasons he took right to the shop instead of going to bed. He sketched it out, decided on dimensions, and figured out what supplies he had and which he lacked. "New project," he said. "Here's my list."

If Brayden left Alaska for good, he wanted Ava to remember him fondly. If he stayed . . . Brayden shook it away. The desire to stay had never been stronger since Mom backed him into this new corner. Four o'clock would come too soon.

"Relax," Brayden said, patting the top of Ava's hand as they sat in his truck in the lodge parking lot. She'd spent the drive through town tapping her ankle boots against the hard plastic floor mats as she dug through her giant purse, but never pulled anything out. "It'll be over before you know it."

Ava looked down at his hand. "Easy for you to say."

"Her bark is way worse than her bite." Brayden squeezed her chilled fingers, hoping she felt the reassurance he extended. "She's tough on the outside, but there's a secret heart of gold underneath it all."

Dad's passing had hardened Mom. She took over the company and threw herself into its success, leaving time for little else. To Brayden's knowledge, Mom had never dated anyone those twenty years after Dad's death. He always suspected her ironclad exterior was her way of protecting her heart.

"Any tips?" Ava asked, pulling away her hand and plunging it back into her purse.

"One."

"Yeah?"

"Don't mention my sister. It's a . . . sore subject."

Ava frowned at him. "Not exactly what I was

looking for, but I'll keep that in mind." She unlocked her phone, typing something into it. *Notes, perhaps?* "No comments about Sarra. Got it."

"Any word yet from your mom?" Brayden asked, fully aware he was stalling. Mom could suffer the few minutes longer. No doubt she was at the table with an open laptop and a glass of pinot noir, completely lost in her inbox.

"No." Ava dropped her phone back into the abyss that was her purse. "I don't know what to make of it. She gets super secretive about gifts, but that's probably the *only* time she ghosts anyone. I wish she'd tell me if she was getting a hotel room. One more day would be *so* nice."

"Ava, everything's going to be fine." He hesitated a moment longer, debating whether to warn her about the surprise Mom was likely to drop on them both. One he wasn't supposed to have prior knowledge about. He decided against it. No matter the obligation or responsibility angle Mom used on him, his answer would be no. He wasn't uprooting his life in mere days to take over the company last minute.

Brayden offered her his arm at the front of the truck, pretending he didn't notice the way the black skirt of her dress swished against her stylish boots at her approach. Despite his pleas for her to be herself, she'd gone out of her way to dress up for this dinner. Wavy curls in her hair, soft color on her eyelids, and even a hint of lip gloss glistened in the reflection of the streetlight.

It didn't matter that several layers of clothing separated them. He could still feel the heat of their interlocked arms.

"That tree is a work of art," Ava said with a nod at the massive Christmas tree in the center of the lobby. It reached more than halfway to the vaulted log ceiling. "Almost puts our tree to shame."

"Nah," Brayden said, leading them off to the side to the dining room. "That one is nice, but our tree is better. It was put together with care and coffee. Lots and lots of coffee."

The smile that graced Ava's lips made him very much want to kiss them. *I wonder if the Whitmore sisters hung any mistletoe.*

He led them to the dining room, spotting his mom in a corner with an open laptop. She looked up at him over the top of her reading glasses.

"Brayden, I didn't know you were bringing a guest." Pamela Young's smile remained frozen in place, but the light dimmed in her eyes at the sight of Ava. Mom wasn't a fan of surprises when she was on the receiving end. She removed her glasses, closed her laptop, and pushed out of her chair.

"Mom," Brayden said. "You came to meet Ava, did you not?" He slipped Ava's arm from his grip to give Mom a purposely overzealous hug. He caught Ava glancing at the exit as he did and cut the embrace short. "Mom, meet Ava Monroe. My girl-friend. She's a local business owner." Brayden turned to Ava. "Ava, meet Pamela Young."

"Nice to finally meet you," said Ava.

Brayden didn't have to be on the receiving end of Mom's handshake to sense the firm and downright scary grip. *Is she squeezing a little too hard on purpose?* If Ava was rattled, she didn't let it show through her perfectly friendly smile. "Welcome to our little town of Sunset Ridge."

"Mom, the table is too small," Brayden said, scanning the dining area for another place to sit. He found an empty two-person table tucked in a corner. Without a server in sight, he took it upon himself to move it and a chair, secretly delighting in Mom's discomfort.

Ava shed her coat and set it on the back of her chair, giving Brayden his first full view of her in the silky black dress that hugged her figure in the most flattering way. "Wow, you look stunning," he said to her in a whisper, meaning it. He hardly saw Ava out of jeans, and only once before in a dress.

"Brayden, you'll need to order another appetizer," Mom said, a flippant edge to her tone. "The crab cakes won't be enough for the three of us."

"We'll be fine, Mom." He pulled out Ava's chair, but she didn't sit.

"Would you excuse me a moment?" she asked. "I need to use the powder room."

"I'll order you a Dr. Pepper," he offered.

Ava gave him a weak smile. One that might fool someone she just met, but not Brayden. Mom was trying to make her uncomfortable, and it seemed in some ways, she was succeeding. "Thanks."

Brayden took his seat after Ava left the dining room and filled his water goblet. "You could try being nice."

"You didn't tell me you invited her." Mom slipped her laptop into its case and set her oversized phone on the table in its place. He used to be like her, he realized. Unable to disconnect for a single moment. There was always an email to answer. A fire to put out. Research to do. Disconnecting from all that offered him a sense of freedom he'd never known and wasn't eager to give up.

"You came to Alaska to meet her."

"I came to Alaska to bring you home. That girl's only after your money."

"She's doesn't know I have any."

Mom raised an eyebrow to that, reaching for her wine glass. "I find that hard to believe."

"I'm just a regular person to this town. Judged by my character, not my bank account balance." Brayden leaned back in his chair, folding his arms over his chest. "You wasted a trip."

"I'm announcing my retirement at the Christmas party next week." She took a slow sip of her wine, no rush in setting the glass on the table before she went on. "You'll be taking over Young Elite Marketing Services effective January first. I need you back now to sign some paperwork and prepare for the transition."

Brayden could hug his sister for the heads-up. Had Mom managed to spring this on him without warning, he would've been blindsided and unable to think everything through. "Maybe I'm not ready to come back."

"It's been almost a year, Brayden. You need to get your head out of the sand. You have responsibilities."

Leaning forward on his elbows, he asked, "Why did you move up your retirement?" He wondered if

Mom would answer his question honestly, or at all. Fear clutched his chest for the briefest moment that maybe she had bad news to share with him. "Is there something I need to know?"

"I'm not dying, if that's what you mean," she answered with a dismissive wave of her hand.

"Then why?"

"It's time."

The answer wasn't good enough. Far from it. But Brayden expected it just the same. That was Mom, always firm in her decisions, but never clear why. She didn't feel she owed anyone a full explanation. He was almost disappointed Ava wasn't here to witness this conversation. She'd understand where he picked up his vague answer habit if she were sitting beside him to witness this exchange.

"I'm leaving on a flight tomorrow evening," Mom continued after they ordered beverages and a second appetizer. "I want you on it with me. I've already booked you a first-class ticket. The corporate Christmas party is Wednesday night. I need you there when I make the announcement."

Chapter Nine

Ava

The moment Ava locked the restroom door behind her, she sank against the cedar planks and forced deep inhales and exhales. It might've helped if Brayden had warned her that his mom was some corporate big wig who'd show up to dinner with a perfectly pressed suit top and skirt, immaculate hair and makeup, and a laptop. Everything about her appearance was crisp and pristine. Exquisite jewelry glistened in the soft lighting. Even her lipstick was the perfect shade, applied in an expert manner.

She understood his warning now. Pamela Young's reading glasses were likely more expensive than Ava's nicest dress. "Deep breaths," she repeated aloud, forcing herself to the sink to splash cool water on her burning cheeks.

Ava was only nervous because she cared that people liked her. She was friendly and kind, and never thought ill of anyone—well, except maybe Ed, but he'd eaten her scarf—and she didn't care for it when someone disliked her without knowing anything about her. The judgmental sweep of Pamela's eyes when she first realized Ava was crashing their dinner was burned into her memory.

Maybe it was for the best she and Brayden had never been on that real date because right now, Ava wasn't certain how she'd handle his mom if they were actually a couple. She still didn't feel welcome. She felt like an intruder.

"But it's fake," she reminded herself. "I just have to play a part." Clearing her throat, she stared intently at herself in the mirror. "Ava Monroe," she said, pushing past her frayed nerves and searching for her confidence, "there's nothing to be afraid of. It's fake. All of it. So what if Brayden's mom is some corporate big shot with eight-hundred-dollar heels? I have bigger problems than Pamela Young. Much bigger problems. You just have to be you. Sweet, friendly, and full of small-town charm and holiday spirit. Your job is to save him from her overbearing ways, just like he's going to save you from Mom. Be. Your. Self."

Confidence restored, Ava marched out the door.

Pivoting around the tight corner toward the dining room, Ava let out a squeak when she nearly plowed someone over. She stumbled a couple of steps back, professing apologies as she saved her purse from slipping all the way off her arm. Then she looked up. "I'm so sor— Wait. Mom?"

"Ava dear!" Mallory Monroe's face lit up brighter than the twelve-foot lodge Christmas tree half a second before she pounced and trapped Ava in a suffocating hug. "I had no idea you'd be here at the lodge. I thought you'd be working." Mom pulled back, leaving her hands cupped on Ava's shoulders tightly enough to warn Ava there was no escape. "Why aren't you working?"

"I'm having dinner with Brayden and his mom." A glance into the dining room warned her she'd stayed gone too long. The expressions between mother and son were much too serious and downright unsettling. Ava took a risk. "Why don't you join us? You have to be starving."

"I don't want to intrude."

Ava swallowed a laugh, hoping Pamela would be

mortified by Mom's Christmas wreath-themed sweater. It wasn't even her selection for the Christmas sweater party, just part of her everyday holiday collection. "We haven't ordered entrees yet. C'mon."

"You must be Mrs. Monroe." Brayden pushed out of his chair so quickly it rocked on its back legs. Appeared she was *just* in the nick of time. "It's a pleasure to meet you."

As expected, Mom tossed both arms around him and squeezed. Brayden recovered his shock quickly and returned the hug with gusto. Ava secretly enjoyed Pamela's annoyance, but she also pitied the woman who didn't appreciate a good, solid family-style hug to a cold handshake.

"It's so good to finally meet the man who's stolen my daughter's heart at long last. I thought she was going to marry that store until you came along. You haven't been letting her work too hard, have you?"

"Holidays are busy, you know," Brayden said, freeing himself of her hold and putting his arm around Ava. "I keep her fueled up on coffee so she can keep up with the booming demand."

"Good, good. Oh, and you must be Brayden's mother. Oh, you're so lovely!" Mom cooed, unde-terred though Pamela hadn't stood. She wrapped her arms around Pamela's shoulders and squeezed, completely ignoring the extended hand and panicked expression of her victim. *Good for you, Mom.*

"I hope you don't mind an extra guest," Ava said to Pamela, taking her seat. "I wasn't sure what time my mom was arriving. Haven't heard from her in hours." Ava pointed her stare at Mom, waiting for an explanation.

"I found a new Christmas CD I just love while I was out shopping. Got a little caught up in the holiday spirit during the drive down. Figured you were busy enough with the store." Mom waved down the server and ordered her usual lemonade. "Wasn't even sure I'd be on my feet the rest of the night, but I've hit my second wind."

"Delightful," Ava mumbled.

"Did Ava tell you about her Christmas baskets that are constantly selling out?" Brayden said.

Ava resisted the urge to stomp on his foot. Now was *not* the time.

"What is he talking about, Ava dear?"

"You'll see them soon enough." Crossing her fingers that she could dodge the Christmas basket discussion for one more day, as Mom was sure to eventually unload her full, unfiltered opinion, Ava switched her attention to Pamela, whose head was bowed low into her phone. "How was your flight, Mrs. Young?"

"Too much turbulence for a red-eye." Pamela slowly tore her gaze away from her screen and lifted her wine glass, showcasing her perfectly manicured red nails.

"Did you see the northern lights?" Mom chimed in.

"No."

"They're supposed to be out tonight," Brayden added. "Mom, you should really see them while you're here. They're one of my favorite things about living in Alaska."

"I doubt I'll be up for those."

Brayden put his arm around Ava's chair, his fingers brushing her shoulder. Tingles erupted on contact, but Ava pretended not to notice them. "Mrs. Young, you can't come all the way to Alaska in the winter and purposely ignore the northern lights. It's practically against the law here."

"I have a conference call in the morning, much earlier than I presume either of you will be awake. I need my sleep."

"Well, perhaps tomorrow night," Ava said.

"They're supposed to be strong through Christmas Eve. Most of the nights include clear skies."

Pamela stared hard at Brayden, and Ava wondered what she missed while hiding out in the bathroom. "Afraid I won't be around for that. I'm flying back tomorrow evening," Pamela finally said, her eyes lifting from her wine glass to her son. "Brayden'll be coming with me."

Ava and Mom both stared at Brayden as if he'd grown a second head. *Is this what I missed earlier?* "Is that true?" she asked in hardly a whisper. His fingers tightened on her shoulder, but she didn't know what it meant. Only that she didn't want him to leave *tomorrow*. He wasn't allowed to abandon her with *no* notice. They had a deal.

"But you'll miss out on so much here, Pamela!" Mom pleaded. "Can't you stay a little while longer? Sunset Ridge is so lovely at Christmastime. Positively magical."

"Our annual company Christmas party is this coming week, and we have lots of preparations to make," Pamela explained, her tone as nonchalant as if they were discussing the weather or the appetizer menu. "It's a huge event, you see. Brayden couldn't possibly miss it. Not with the big news we have to share."

"I'm not going." Brayden's tone was cool, confident, and equally as nonchalant. So much calmer than Ava with her erratically beating heart. *What big news?*

"Of course you are."

"No, I'm not." He waited as the server placed plates of crab cakes and lobster rolls on the table. Ava studied his expression for hints of what he had up his sleeve, because she could sense it was something. She wished for once the man wasn't so darn secretive. The suspense was killing her.

"Everything is already settled, Brayden," Pamela said between gritted teeth after orders were placed. "You're needed at home."

"*This* is my home." His tone was quiet, but firm. Commanding. It gave Ava chills of admiration. "If you want me to even consider taking over the company, you'll stick around through Christmas. See why I love it here so much."

"I can't—"

"I won't entertain leaving until you understand what it is I'd be giving up." Brayden lifted a crab cake onto his appetizer plate, still calm as could be. But panic seized Ava as she realized the gravity of those words. Brayden might leave. For good. Her stomach tied in knots at the thought of losing her duplex neighbor . . . *forever*. It was Elsie. She was saddened by the thought of never seeing the golden again. Nothing more. *Right?*

"I have meetings. Conference calls."

"Reschedule them," Brayden shot back. "It's nearly Christmas. You need to get out of your inbox and see what this town is all about. You're not allowed to hide out in your lodge room the whole time you're here."

"Oh, you couldn't possibly do that!" Mom cooed. "I'd be happy to show you around. You can't leave until you've had Willamina's fresh halibut chowder or snow-shoed up to the best lookout point in town. The view is stunning enough to make a person cry. And those northern lights, I promise you've never seen anything like them. And that's not to mention all the Christmas—"

"We can discuss this tomorrow," Pamela interjected, her gaze fixed on Brayden.

"There's nothing more to discuss. I have obligations here. A wedding to attend and a festive Christmas sweater event Ava's family puts on every year." He looked at Ava, his eyes sparkling with victory. "I'm certain I have the winning sweater."

Any attempts to convince herself that this was all an act were futile. Ava was falling for her fake boyfriend, and she wasn't quite certain how to stop it from happening.

"Pamela, you *must* join in! I brought extra sweaters if you need one. It's a family tradition, not to mention such a hoot!"

"I'm sorry to be a spoilsport, but I can't possibly stay. The company Christmas party—"

"Let Sarra manage it this year."

Ava's eyes widened before she could recover her shock. Pamela didn't miss it either. Darn Brayden and his inability to confide the important things. Of course, he was the one who told her not to mention his sister, and then he did it himself. What wasn't he saying?

"She doesn't need anything else added to her plate."

"Maybe you don't keep her plate full enough." Brayden slipped his phone from his jacket pocket. "Should I call her and ask?"

"Sounds like it's all settled." Mom's smile was dangerously cheerful as she fumbled with her phone. "I'm going to enter the four of us into the local Christmas cookie-baking contest. If you don't have a favorite recipe," she said to Pamela, eyes still fixed on her screen, "I have a few you can choose from. Winning team gets five hundred town bucks."

"I don't bake—"

"There! We're all entered. Tuesday evening." Mom dropped her phone back in her purse, refusing to meet Ava's assessing gaze. The woman didn't know how to take down a photo posted on Facebook, but she entered the *four* of them into the baking contest with lightning speed? There would be words later.

"Sounds fantastic." Brayden eased back against his chair, his smile smug yet somehow charming and butterfly-worthy.

Before Pamela could object, the server appeared with a full tray, handing out entrees. For several minutes, conversation evaporated completely. Ava had been meaning to try out Whitmore Patio since it opened, but time always seemed to work against her. Then the budget. But she wished she'd treated herself before now, because the food was amazing. The same Whitmore sister who originally shot down her Christmas basket pitch before she gave her a maybe—Tessa—was a professional chef who left behind the big-city life to open the charming lodge restaurant.

"This food is amazing!" Mom exclaimed. "Makes me want to move back."

Ava nearly choked on her final bite of mushroom

risotto. "How's Jamie?" she asked, eager to remind Mom why she couldn't possibly leave Minnesota.

"Cranky." Mom cut the last of her salmon. "Course, when I was thirty-eight weeks pregnant with you, I was a grizzly bear, too. You're not comfortable, you don't sleep, and your back hurts *all* the time."

"Jamie's my youngest sister," Ava explained.

"You'll find out soon enough if this one decides to put a ring on your finger," Mom added with her overly cheerful smile.

"Mom!"

"Ladies, it's been a lovely evening," Brayden said, scooting his chair back. "But Ava and I both have work to do tonight *and* early tomorrow morning. We have to get ahead to make the baking contest, you see."

"And the Christmas sweater party!" Mom added. "Monday at four thirty." She looked at Ava in apology. "Jamie refused to let Trey stay up too late. Can you work that out in your store schedule?"

Ava couldn't get her coat on fast enough. "I hired Rilee, remember? She's happy to cover as often as I need her, as long as it doesn't interfere with the wedding."

"I don't know how you afford this," Mom muttered.

"We'll see you tomorrow," Ava said. "Mrs. Young, it was nice meeting you. Let Mom show you the sights. Sunset Ridge is a wonderful little town. You should try to enjoy it while you're here."

She and Brayden made it as far as the Christmas tree centered in the lobby before they were stopped again. "Ava, wait!" Cadence called after them, rushing their way. "Do you still have those Christmas baskets?"

The tension from the awkward family dinner dissipated, until she spotted the moms exiting the dining room. Ava discreetly shuffled back one slow step at a time until she and Brayden were nearly hidden beneath a ledge. If she didn't need these sales so desperately, she'd make an excuse to bolt. "Yes, I do."

"I talked it over with my sisters, and we decided they would be lovely gifts for our lodge guests staying over the holidays." Cadence revealed a notebook, flipping through dozens of pages before she found her spot. Unfortunately, Mom's curiosity was clearly piqued, and she was heading over. "I made a list of guests staying between now and Christmas. You know, how many, which ones have kids. That sort of thing, since you offer different sizes."

"Did you want to email me your order?" Ava suggested as Mom paused to admire the tree, tugging on Pamela's arm and pointing at one of the ornaments.

"I have it right here. I need them as soon as you can deliver. Tomorrow morning, if you can manage it."

Ava had a few assembled baskets taking residence on her couch and dining table. Though the dinner had wiped her energy and she craved nothing more than some hot cocoa and a fuzzy blanket, she could work tonight. Every sale mattered.

"Tomorrow morning is doable," Brayden answered, placing his arm around her waist as the moms glanced at them together. Ava was more worried about the mischievous twinkle in Mom's eyes than Pamela's unconvinced scowl. "Even if Ava has to hire an elf to make it happen."

"Wonderful!" Cadence ripped out a notebook page and handed it to Ava. "These are the quantities of each. I'll have a check ready for you in the morning."

Hope filled Ava at the total number. *Thirty-two.* It wasn't enough to save the store, but it was definitely more than she'd hoped from the lodge. "We'll drop these off in the morning."

"Please use the back door. We don't want to spoil the surprise for our guests."

"Of course."

As Cadence stepped away, Mom dashed toward them. Pamela lurked near the tree, preoccupied with her phone. "Please let me take a picture. I won't post it on social media."

"You expect me to believe that?" Ava shot back, not sad at all when Brayden pulled her closer to him. Fake relationship or not, she enjoyed his warmth and the comfort it brought. Their friendship was rekindling. She still had dozens of questions she'd fire at him the second they got home, but in this one moment, she felt calm.

"Just one," Mom pleaded.

"Fine."

"Get closer together, you two."

"Just do it," Brayden whispered against her ear. "The sooner she gets her picture, the sooner your elf-for-hire can get to work."

"There's that beautiful smile," Mom cooed, snapping at least ten photos. Maybe fifteen. "Maybe you two should take your coats off—"

"Mom, don't push your luck."

"Oh, look!" Mom pointed to something above them, and it wasn't until Ava looked straight up that she realized her grave mistake. Mistletoe hung off the ledge. How had she *not* noticed it earlier? It had occurred to her many times that they might need to kiss to make things convincing, but when faced with the reality without time to prepare, her panic returned.

Brayden caressed her cheek. "If we don't do this, it might blow our cover," he said, the low timbre of his voice sending shivers throughout her body despite the crackling fire nearby. "It won't be so bad, Ava. I promise."

He bowed his head, brushing her lips with his own before she had time to object. Not that she *could* object with Mom so eagerly awaiting them to fulfill the silly holiday tradition. But the camera snaps and Mom worries gave way as the sensation of his lips moving against her own took over. Ava felt dizzy as his kiss deepened. She fell into its magic, breathless when Brayden pulled away.

It wasn't the potency of that kiss alone that had her rattled. It was the urge to do it again.

Chapter Ten

BRAYDEN

"Is that the last one?" Ava asked, nodding at the basket in Brayden's hands.

"The last one that'll fit in the truck." Brayden trotted down the stairs to the front door, waiting for Ava to follow. She'd spent several hours last night assembling baskets after the moms were effectively appeased and dodged. At least, the glow of the living room light suggested as much. She'd turned down his offer of help, which was just as well. Not only did he have three orders to fill, he wanted to start on her desk.

And they both needed some space after that kiss.

It was more astounding than he ever dared dream it would be, especially for one intended only to maintain their cover. His lips still buzzed from the memory of it.

"I think I made close to a hundred of those last night," she said, tying her scarf around her neck and following him outside. If she was affected by that kiss, she wasn't acting like it. Everything with Ava seemed back to business as usual. "But I'll need to make more. Guess I've got a *good* problem on my hands."

Already this morning, Ava made a delivery to the property management office and he dropped off two dozen to the lodge. The rest of the baskets packed into their vehicles would replace sold inventory in the store. The only damper was that Brayden's contact, originally due to show up late this afternoon, rescheduled for Monday morning. *Oh, well.* It was too much to hope they'd save the store before sundown today.

"You operate pretty well under pressure," he said, handing over a final basket.

Ava just laughed in response, closing her passenger door with care, her eyes fixed on the precarious arrangement of baskets inside. "I haven't been calm one solitary minute in"—she tapped her chin—"three months? Maybe four."

He wished he could write a check now for the loan balance and let this madness be over, if only to give Ava a day of rest. A day not filled with constant worry, but of peace. A day she might finally enjoy to its fullest. "This was a great idea," Brayden praised. "One made under pressure. You're no quitter, Ava Monroe. That might be what I like most about you."

The cold could be blamed for the flush of her cheeks, but Brayden suspected it was his compliment.

"We better get going. I don't know how long I have before Mom descends on the store and tries to rearrange all my displays and change half my prices."

Brayden let out a laugh.

"You think I'm kidding." Ava hurried around the side of her car, and he caught them both scanning for Ed. "I'm almost surprised he's not here," she added, gloveless fingertips on her door handle. "He's been great at making me late for pretty much everything this week. It's almost a little ominous, to be honest."

He drove his truck, following Ava in her car. They could transport more baskets this way, and at the rate they'd been selling, having the extra inventory at the store was for her benefit. At last count, she was up to over a hundred sales. As phenomenal as that number was, it was still a small fraction of what she needed to move before Christmas, no matter how many other items were bought up.

Brayden carried a load of baskets to the front of the Forget Me Not, holding the door for Ava with his back to it. Her grateful smile faded seconds after stepping inside. Mallory Monroe whisked around the store, stringing lights on top of the shelves, and singing off-key with the Christmas music. *This can't be good*.

"Mom, what are you doing?"

"Decorating, Ava dear. Isn't it lovely?"

Brayden quietly carried the baskets to the display area, noticing a void of customers and only Rilee Harris manning the front counter. Though Mrs. Baker, the second-grade teacher, had been pulling out of a parking spot when he pulled into one.

"I already decorated," Ava countered, shedding her coat and laying it behind the counter.

"Well, you didn't put any lights around the shelves. Thought I'd add the finishing touches since I'm here."

He felt like a traitor, marching back out into the cold for more gift baskets, but what could he do? It was on his third trip in that he spotted Mallory in the corner ogling the baskets while Ava showed Rilee something at the register. "Ava, what are these?"

Ava murmured something to Rilee before scooting out from behind the counter and marching toward the display corner. "Gift baskets, Mother. What do they look like?"

"Aren't they wonderful?" Brayden chimed in, putting his arm around Ava's shoulders and pulling her against him. Kissing her on the temple was probably a bit much, but he blamed it on looking the part. He hoped to prevent an all-out war that already raged in Ava's eyes. He'd have to figure out a way to get Mallory out of the store so Ava could run her business without interference. "They're selling like hotcakes."

"We've never done gift baskets before," Mallory commented.

He felt Ava tense. "No, *we* haven't."

Mallory lifted a small basket, searching the bottom. "Who made these?"

"These were all Ava," Brayden boasted. "I helped a little. But all this is Ava's creation. I just followed some very detailed instructions. With their unique qualities, you'd never guess she's got this down to a science. The customers can't get enough of them. The lodge ordered several for their guests. I bet there's a basket waiting for you on your bed as we speak."

Ava offered him a smile, her intoxicating peppermint aroma drifting around him, threatening to distract his main mission. It reminded him of the mistletoe-induced kiss they shared only last night. Why couldn't Mallory hang more of *that* instead of lights?

"You're underpricing these," Mallory warned. "They should be *at least* ten dollars more. Probably twelve."

"Not this close to Christmas," Ava said coolly, folding her arms. "I wouldn't move nearly as many if I raised the price. I did my research, Mom, just like you taught me. And the profit margin on them is more than you might think. I was *very* resourceful."

Mallory stretched her neck over Ava's shoulder, glancing at Rilee. "Are you planning to give out holiday bonuses?" she asked in a loud whisper.

"Mrs. Monroe," Brayden said, slipping his arm off Ava's shoulder and placing it on Mallory's. "Have you had a chance to see everything your talented daughter has done with the store since you last visited?" He urged her away from the corner despite her obvious objections and slyly lulled her into a tour. Mallory only looked back at Ava once before he sucked her in, using his best sales tactics. It was easy to do with how intimately familiar he was with most of the inventory. He owned more items than not. "These northern lights mugs are my favorite." Brayden pointed. "Ava tells me they're one of her tried-and-true products."

"I first sold those twenty-two years ago. They're always a big hit with the tourists."

"The locals, too," Brayden said with a wink. "I have four in my cupboard, and I've sent a dozen to my grandma in Texas to share with her friends."

Mallory cooed in approval, but her gaze drifted back toward the basket display. Her smile faltered, and Brayden knew he had to do something. Mallory meant well, of that he was certain. But Ava had enough on her plate without added pressure. The whole point of the fake relationship was to save each other from their mothers. Since his was preoccupied in her lodge room all morning with conference calls she refused to reschedule, he could do Ava this kindness. With any luck, he'd have the two moms paired up and sightseeing by lunch.

"I have something I need to ask you," he said, keeping his voice hushed beneath the broadcasted Christmas tune.

Mallory's eyes lit. "Ask away," she responded in a conspiratorial whisper.

"That desk in Ava's office. Is it a family heirloom?"

She snorted. "That rickety thing? Hardly. I bought that at a store closing one of my first years running the shop. I'm surprised Ava still keeps it around. Why do you ask?"

Brayden snuck a glance at Ava, ushering Mallory into the opposite corner of the store that held women's sweaters and a display of gloves. He wondered if Ava'd find it funny or offensive if he bought her a pair for Christmas. He made a mental note to pick up one later when she wasn't working so he could find out. "I don't know if Ava mentioned it, but I'm a woodworker. I make coffee tables, dressers, end tables. That sort of thing."

"How lovely."

Brayden bowed his head deeper, lowering his voice further. "I'm making Ava a desk for Christmas. I've only just started on it, but I wonder if you might take a look at the design. Make any suggestions before I get to the point of no return. But if your schedule is too full—"

"Oh, I can spare a little time for consulting. I do

know her so well. We worked side-by-side for over a decade. Plus, I *am* her mom, you know."

"I knew I asked the right person." Brayden slipped behind the counter, procuring Mallory's coat. As he helped her into it, he caught Ava's gaze. "I'm going to give your mom a tour of my wood-working shop. Let her know who her daughter's really tangled up with."

"You two have fun." The relief in Ava's voice was clear as a cloudless sky, making him feel he'd finally gotten something right when it came to his neighbor.

"I'll see you this evening, Ava dear," Mallory added as she buttoned up. "Having lunch with Pam. Promised to change her life with that halibut chowder. She doesn't know it yet, but we're also taking a stroll through the park to look at the holiday-themed ice sculptures. Told Chase I'd decorate his house tonight." Mallory rushed to the door to catch up with Brayden, but she wasn't finished. "Tomorrow I have presents to wrap for the sweater party. And the lodge is having a book club late in the afternoon. Ran into Marianne Baxter and she told me I just *had* to come. Maybe we can grab some pie tomorrow evening?"

"Sure thing," Ava said with a wave. "Have fun."

"Should we stop for coffee?" Brayden asked Mallory as he held the door open. Ava mouthed *thank you* before he let it fall shut. Her grateful smile was all the reward he needed. He couldn't image a day without it.

"That would be wonderful!"

Brayden offered her his arm. "Too beautiful a day to drive a block."

"Indeed it is. You just might be a keeper, Brayden Young."

Armed with coffee, Brayden had Mallory follow him back to the duplex and purposely parked in the front so she could admire the Christmas tree in Ava's window. Because his focus was elsewhere, he didn't notice the car parked outside his woodworking shop until he set Elsie free and they went around back.

"Oh, good," Mallory said. "I was hoping to run into your mother. I knocked on her door earlier, but I should've paid attention to the do-not-disturb sign on the knob."

"I think she had a conference call this morning." Brayden shoved his hands in his pockets, uncertain what was to come of this unexpected visit. Another ambush? Or had Mom relented and decided to stay in Sunset Ridge a few more days?

Elsie trotted happily through the snow, flurries catching in her coat. The second Mom's car door opened, the dog ran straight for her. Brayden didn't bother hiding his smile as Mom shrieked. "She's friendly," he called out. "Unless you're a tree branch."

"What a lovely dog. I bet Ava just dotes on her, doesn't she?" Mallory asked. If he wasn't mistaken, she was fighting a laugh at Mom's apparent discomfort with Elsie's eager greeting.

"Elsie sneaks over to Ava's back door every morning for treats."

"Brayden, call your dog off!" Mom hollered.

He whistled for Elsie, and the golden momentarily froze before she trotted toward him.

"Such a well-behaved dog," Mallory said, bending to welcome Elsie with mitten-clad pats. The complete opposite of his mom. "I'm a cat person myself, but this sweet girl could sway me."

"Would you believe I got her at a shelter a year ago? Someone moved away and—"

"That's horrible," Mallory said, catching up to him. "Who would do such a thing? When we retired to Minnesota, we took Mittens and Smokey with us. Never would've dreamed of leaving them behind. Pets are family."

Brayden put an arm around Mallory, mostly to annoy his own mom. But her scowl only lasted two seconds before her phone robbed her attention yet again. Another email. Another fire to put out. "I think you and I are going to get along *very* well, Mrs. Monroe."

"Oh, Mallory please. Mrs. Monroe is my mother-in-law."

"I'll get the stove going in just a minute." Unlocking his woodworking shop, he held the door open. Not unsurprisingly, Mom wasn't dressed for an Alaskan winter. Her toes in those high heels had to be frozen solid. "Ava sells boots at the Forget Me Not," he directed at his mom. "You should pick up a pair."

"We need to talk."

He kept his back pointed at her as he worked the stove, bringing it to life as Elsie trotted to her favorite window lookout via the steps and perch he'd built her this past summer. "Mallory, the plans for that desk are on that table over there," he said with a nod. "Look them over. Let me know what you think. I'm going to show my mom the sanding room."

Brayden led Mom into the smaller of the two working areas, closed the door, then waited.

Mom glanced at her phone, and with great

struggle in her eyes, dropped it into her coat pocket. "If I agree to stay the weekend, will you come home with me? There's a Sunday night flight—"

"That wasn't the agreement."

"I can't stay beyond that." Mom used her firm tone that let an employee know they'd overstepped their bounds, but it didn't have the same effect on Brayden. He'd expected her to negotiate. It's what she taught him, after all. "The Christmas party—"

"I already offered you a perfectly acceptable solution."

Mom scoffed. "Sarra?"

He wished he didn't know that Sarra was set on leaving the company. Keeping that secret frustrated him, but he wouldn't betray Sarra's trust—even if it meant Mom was about to lose not only her daughter, but one of her most valuable employees. "Yes, Sarra."

"She doesn't have enough experience."

"She would *gain* experience if you granted her the opportunity." Brayden checked the wood stacked against the wall, wishing he led a messier existence so he could keep his hands busy. Mom could be one of the most stubborn people he knew, and it was going to cost her so much. "Either you stay through Christmas and we revisit this retirement conversation then, or you get on your flight now and find a new CEO to replace you."

"Fine, you win."

Brayden was certain he heard her wrong.

"I'll stay through Christmas. But, we *will* have this conversation on Christmas Day. I've been more than patient with you this last year." Some emotion Brayden couldn't quite pin flashed across Mom's face. *Pain?* "I'm retiring whether you like it or not, and this company needs to stay in the family. It's what your father would've wanted."

"You're joining in the Christmas festivities."

"I'm not doing a baking contest."

Feeling victorious, he slipped his arm around Mom's shoulder and led her back to the door. "Oh, but you are, Mother." He found Mallory on the cot, snuggling Elsie. "I even picked you out an apron."

Chapter Eleven

AVA

"Mom, what are you doing to my kitchen?" Ava dropped her purse on the couch, too stunned at the baking explosion happening in her cramped kitchen to unwrap her scarf. When she agreed to let her mom come over early to prepare for the Christmas sweater party, this was not what she had in mind.

"I'm practicing for the baking contest tomorrow." Mom rinsed a metal measuring cup in the sink and towel-dried it. Practicing was hardly the word Ava would use to describe the array of mixing bowls and dozens of cookies taking over every inch of surface from the breakfast bar to the dining table, to the window ledges. "I can't come all this way and lose to Tillie Grant."

"Don't you mean *we*?"

Mom flashed her a smile before she dunked that same measuring cup into a bag of white sugar. "Of course, Ava dear."

Overheated no doubt from an oven that had likely been running nonstop for hours, Ava finally shed her coat and scarf and tossed them over the back of the couch. The Christmas sweater party was in less than an hour, and Mom hadn't done a thing to get ready for it. *Guess I'll text Brayden to help.*

Ava: SOS. Come over ten minutes ago.
Brayden: Coffee run. Be there soon.
Ava: Get me a double shot plz?
Brayden: You got it

"Texting your boyfriend?" Mom cooed in the same tone she had when Ava was a teenager mooning over a boy.

"He's grabbing coffee." All weekend, Ava had been free of her mom outside of a quick pie date. Brayden had worked some sort of magic to pair the moms together and keep them occupied. She never expected Pamela to go for it, but Mom had sent photos throughout the weekend of their adventures. Despite the mountain of work that never ended, Ava felt the pressure ease those two days.

She hadn't seen much of Brayden, as he was working on some last-minute order. It shouldn't seem like a downside. And her heart certainly shouldn't flutter the way it did now at the prospect of seeing him. They weren't together. *But what if we were?*

"I do hope he's bringing that sweet Elsie with him. I'm tempted to smuggle her back to Minnesota in my carry-on."

"Elsie." Ava spun in a circle, overwhelmed by the number of cookies *everywhere*. "I have containers downstairs," she said. "Let me grab them. Elsie on sugar is . . . you don't want to know." She scurried down the stairs, diving into the spare bedroom half-filled with holiday totes in search of her snowman-decorated Tupperware. "No way I have enough," she muttered, stacking them in her arms.

It wasn't until Ava was at the foot of the stairs that she noticed the cracked door to the garage.

"Oh, no."

Ava set the wobbly stack of containers on the bottom step and approached the garage with caution. It didn't matter that she'd assembled more than two hundred baskets. Mom snooping in her garage with all the remaining supplies wasn't good. It was downright terrifying.

Flipping on the light, Ava cautiously moved through the narrow aisles, searching for anything out of place. A clue that Mom had invaded and was coping with her overly excessive baking. "That could be it," Ava muttered. Mom might've figured out the dire financial situation of the store and was too afraid to say anything. She was never one to sit still when anxious.

But nothing was moved.

"Maybe I got lucky," she murmured.

"Ava?" Mom called, her voice much too close.

With what she could only consider to be ninja moves she'd stored deep in her subconscious for a perilous situation such as this, Ava weaved back to the door. Flipping the lock, she yanked it closed, nearly bumping noses with Mom.

"What are you doing?" Mom asked, craning her neck over Ava's shoulder as if she could see through the solid door.

"Thought I had more containers out there." Ava shimmied around her, picking up the stack she'd left behind. "I guess we'll have to make do with these." When Mom stood unmoving, staring at the garage door, Ava added, "You have to help me put these away before Elsie shows up. They're five minutes out."

"Is there anything you want to tell me, Ava dear?" Mom asked once upstairs, caution in that tone.

"Nope."

"You're sure?"

The chime of the doorbell saved her. "I better grab the door for Brayden. His hands'll be full." But when she pulled the door open, Kinley stood on the other side, decked out in a fabulously horrendous reindeer sweater.

"Hope I'm not too early."

Ava yanked her inside by the wrist, relieved at the interruption. Three more days. That was all Ava had to survive. If she could make enough in sales by Christmas Eve, she would never have to tell Mom anything was wrong. "You're just in time."

"Kinley, how wonderful to see you, dear!" Mom wrapped Kinley in her famous suffocating hug. "Do you want to try some cookies? I'm practicing for our mother-daughter team. Contest is tomorrow, you know. Did you enter this year?"

"I'm a little swept up in wedding planning,"

Kinley admitted, accepting the full dessert plate of cookies. "But I'm happy to be a guinea pig today."

"Where's that hunky man of yours?" Mom asked.

"Just finished his shift. He'll be over soon."

"Mom, why don't you get the kitchen in order?" Ava suggested. "Kinley can help me get everything cleaned up before everyone else gets here." She swiped a snickerdoodle from Kinley's plate and took a bite.

"What do you need?" Kinley asked between bites of her own.

"I need to put all the extra baskets and decorations in the spare room. I'll deal with them later." Ava grabbed all she could and rushed down the narrow hall to a room she had thankfully locked before allowing Mom access to her house. The room was stuffed fuller than the garage, mostly with Christmas baskets.

"Just how many of these baskets did you make?" Kinley asked inside the room.

"A few dozen."

"Looks more like a few hundred to me."

Worried Mom might eavesdrop, she closed the door, barricading them inside the spare bedroom. "Don't make a big deal about it, okay? Mom gets nosy. Christmas is almost here, and then—" Ava cut herself off, realizing what confession was about to slip out. "Never mind. I just don't want Mom being overly snoopy."

"Are you sure everything's okay? We're *best* friends. You know you can tell me anything." Kinley pinned her with a concerned look, making Ava squirm. She was close to saving the store. With the massive order a businesswoman from Anchorage placed today, she held hope. Real hope. Ava still had no idea how she was going to transport seventy-five of them to Anchorage by Wednesday at lunch in time for a corporate Christmas party, but she would figure it out. She always did.

"It's fine," Ava finally said when Kinley didn't budge. "Just a little worn out from the holidays. It's my busiest time of year, outside of festival weekends in the summer. Can you please just drop it?" She asked the last in a soft plea.

Kinley lifted her hands in surrender. "Okay, okay. The topic is dropped."

"Thank you." But when Ava attempted to maneuver around Kinley for the door, she was blocked yet again. "We don't have much time—"

"I want to ask you a favor." Judging by Kinley's ominous tone, Ava wasn't going to like said favor.

She folded her arms and waited. "Talk to Laurel. Do it for me, please. I want my two best friends to get along for my wedding."

"Your wedding is six months away."

Kinley's frown deepened. "That's why I want you two to sort everything out well in advance. Consider it my Christmas wish. Just pick up the phone and call her, Ava. She misses you. I know you two have a lot of history—"

"That's one way to put it." Ava didn't mean to sound like a spoiled brat, but why did Laurel have to be brought into this conversation? "Kinley, she *married* Chase without telling me. They snuck away without telling a soul they were even dating, and came back married. If that weren't bad enough, she dumped him a few months later and disappeared."

"And she's been trying to make amends ever since."

"I'm not doing this right now." Ava couldn't handle one more thing on her precariously over-flowing plate. Laurel least of all. "Ask me after New Year's. I'll reconsider then." *After I know the fate of the store.*

"This really can't wait. Ava, she's—"

Rapid knocking startled them both. Ava startled, her feet tripping. She nearly took out half a dozen baskets, but Kinley's quick hand saved her balance. "Girls, are you in there? Chase is here."

Ava darted out of the room before Kinley could press the matter further. She would think about her former best friend later. There simply wasn't time— or energy—to deal with it before Christmas. She quickly gathered the remaining clutter and stuffed it away, hiding away in her own bedroom for a few minutes.

While she changed into her Christmas sweater, Elsie nosed at the door and nudged her way inside.

"Hey, girl." Ava knelt and hugged the golden. Her grip was a little too tight, if Elsie's squirming was any indication, but Ava needed it. Elsie licked her cheek in apparent understanding. "If you weren't so perfect, I'd adopt a dog myself. But you're irre-placeable."

Gentle rapping drew her gaze to the ajar door. "I come bearing coffee."

Ava's stomach fluttered instantly at the sight of Brayden and those kind, sparkling eyes. She was so enamored by his smile and the chiseled cut of his jaw covered with a freshly trimmed beard that it took her several embarrassingly long seconds to notice the sweater.

"Holy jingle bells." Ava popped to her feet and

rounded the bed to get a better look at the green and red atrocity covered in cats, Christmas trees, and yarn. Yarn she could pull away with her fingertips. "This is . . . amazing. Has Mom seen it yet?"

"Not yet."

Ava dropped her fingers from the yarn and accepted the coffee. She stole a glance at his lips in passing, the urge to revisit that mistletoe oddly overwhelming. The two days apart felt like two weeks. Maybe two months. It didn't make any sense. She and Brayden were friends, neighbors. He might leave. *For good.*

"Better get out there," Brayden said. "I think everyone's here."

Closing the bedroom door behind her, Ava felt her stress dissipate. Seemed every time Brayden was near, she felt a little calmer. Like the world wasn't so heavy on her shoulders. It made her sad to think he might move to Texas to take over his mom's company.

"Ava," Mom called before she could emerge from the hallway. "Chase needs your Wi-Fi password! We need to get Skype up and going before Trey's bedtime."

The living and dining rooms were filled—Mom, Chase, Kinley, Ryder, Brayden, Elsie, and even

Pamela, in Mom's Christmas sweater from last year. Her heart felt full, despite the chaos and roar of voices. Mom kept hurrying to the kitchen, then stopping only feet away because she remembered something else.

It was oddly wonderful. A reminder that her house was usually too empty. Too quiet.

"I'm glad you forced me to get that tree," Ava said to Brayden, bumping him with her shoulder. His cologne, some mix of sandalwood, sawdust, and peppermint if she wasn't mistaken, intoxicated Ava. Made her want to curl up in his arms on the couch.

"Sometimes you just have to trust."

"Hello?" Mom hollered into the computer screen.

"Grandma!" Trey's young voice exclaimed, making the entire room smile. He filled the screen with his face. Frosting smeared his lips and one cheek. Ava doubted that kid was heading to bed anytime soon.

"You get to visit often?" Brayden asked Ava from their spot in the back of the room.

"I've only met Trey twice. Once when he was first born, and once when Jamie came to Alaska the summer he was two. He's a great kid."

"I know you love that store, but you should make

the time to see them. Easier for you to hand over the store to trusted employees for a few days than it is for your sister to travel with a little one."

"About to be *two* little ones."

"Do you want kids?" Brayden asked.

The question caught Ava off-guard. Not that she hadn't thought about having a family of her own—of course she wanted that—but that Brayden was the one asking. If she wasn't careful, she was going to forget this whole relationship was fake. "I—"

"Quiet everyone!" Mom announced. "It's time to get started. Grab some cookies, find a seat, and I'll explain how it all works in just a minute."

Brayden ushered Ava to the couch, his hand warm on the small of her back. They sat smooshed together so Kinley and Ryder fit on the other end. But she didn't mind being this close to Brayden. She enjoyed his warmth, and leaned into him when he put his arm around her. "This really is a ridiculous sweater," she said, playing again with a loose strand of yarn. "Where did you find it?"

"I took a slight detour when I made that coffee table delivery the other day."

"I thought that was in Girdwood."

"It was."

Mom hushed the crowd once again, leaving Ava

to speculate. Had Brayden driven the extra thirty miles to Anchorage to find the perfect Christmas sweater? She remembered the tip Chase gave him the other day, but never thought for a moment that Brayden would take it seriously.

"Here's how this works," Mom explained, handing around homemade cards and pencils. "Everyone gets a turn to strut their stuff and show off their sweater. The rest will rate the sweaters." She went on to explain a simple points system and how they'd determine the winner. Ava stopped listening almost immediately, not only because she already knew the rules, but because she was much too distracted with Brayden sitting so close.

Suddenly the idea of telling the moms that this whole relationship was a joke on them wasn't appealing.

It was depressing.

Yes, Ava was in trouble when it came to Brayden Young, and she had no idea what to do about it. Especially if he moved away to Texas and never looked back.

Chapter Twelve

BRAYDEN

"You're eating Fairbanks Fudge, aren't you?" Brayden accused his mom as she locked her lodge room, unsuccessfully hiding the flavored chunk of fudge she'd stuffed in her mouth, nor the twinkle of delight in her eyes as she savored the bite.

"So what if I am?" she asked while chewing. "It's good."

"That came from the Forget Me Not Boutique."

She pretended to busy herself on her phone, but Brayden could see at a glance that she had no new emails. "I'm well aware."

He draped his arm around Mom, mostly to

annoy her, as they made their way down the hall. She was never one for heavy physical affection, but she didn't shimmy out of his hold. The past couple of days had no doubt been good for her. He couldn't recall the last vacation Mom took, and even when she did get out of town, she always brought the office with her.

Pairing the moms together was a risk, considering their highly opposite personalities. But Brayden hoped it had paid off. He couldn't remember the last time Mom seemed so relaxed instead of on edge.

"I still don't understand why we have to be in a baking contest," she said once outside. "I don't bake."

"You used to." Brayden opened the passenger door and offered Mom a hand into the truck. "Don't you remember?"

"That was a long time ago," Mom said, fastening her seat belt and leaving Brayden to close the door. He remembered Christmases in the kitchen, baking for days. Not just cookies, but fudge, caramel corn, Chex mix, and dipped pretzels. Dad had been the workaholic in those days. Had his passing robbed her of simple pleasures? Mom was always heavily involved in the company before Dad was gone, but she had managed balance.

Seemed she needed a reminder. "I have three

recipes," Brayden said once in the truck. He reached into the interior chest pocket of his coat and pulled out the cards. "Pick one."

"Now?"

Brayden rolled to a stop at a four-way intersection, waiting for another car to go. Its wheels spun on the icy street for several seconds before it found traction. It reminded him of Ava, a lifelong Alaskan, driving a car with worn-down snow tires. He wished she'd let him take care of her. But convincing Ava it wasn't about the money would be harder than convincing Mom he wasn't the one best suited to run her company. "We have roughly ten minutes to stop at the grocery store to pick up our ingredients. We can't miss the competition briefing or we get disqualified."

"I never really cared for those peanut butter ones with the chocolate center." Mom slipped that card to the bottom of the stack. "And we can't do snickerdoodles," she said dismissively. "Mallory's making those."

"Santa's Whiskers it is," Brayden decided, pulling into a spot outside the store.

Mom peered through the windshield into the cozy grocery store. "Can I wait here?"

"No." Brayden hopped out of the truck, not

giving her time to argue. Mallory had thawed Mom out of her ice-cold shell these past couple of days; anyone with eyes could see that. But it was up to Brayden to do the rest. He wanted her to understand why he couldn't leave this place without leaving a piece of his heart behind. Inside the store, she'd see how many people greeted him by name and asked about Elsie.

"I'll have you know I rescheduled a conference call for you," Mom said, trotting behind him in boots. Either she finally broke down and bought a pair of her own or Mallory outfitted her. At least Brayden didn't have to worry about frostbite.

He ushered her inside. "You should reschedule a few more."

As expected, half a dozen people greeted Brayden. He spared enough time to introduce them to his mom. If they weren't in a hurry to make it to the competition, he would've forced Mom to endure some visiting. One of the patrons had purchased a set of his very first nightstands. Small-town folks loved to chat, and they *cared* about one another. Not something he'd ever found in the city.

"You two better hurry," Aimee at the register said, holding out Brayden's receipt to him. "You'll be late for the briefing. You can't compete if you miss that."

"How do so many people know you?" Mom asked on the drive to the town hall. "Every single person in that store stopped to talk to you. It's the most astounding thing I've seen in quite a while."

"I've been here almost a year. I'm one of them now. That's how the whole small-town thing works." He parked the truck, cut the ignition, and reached into the back seat for their supplies. "We better get inside before they start without us."

"Are you sure we have to do this?"

"It'll be fun. Like when Sarra and I were kids, the kitchen was covered in flour, and Christmas music blasted on the loudest setting." Brayden followed Mom inside the town hall building, decked out in heavy greenery and lights. They checked in at the door and proceeded into the main competition area. A dozen stations were staged throughout the small but well-organized area, each equipped with mixers, measuring cups, and baking sheets. In the middle, rows of chairs were lined up, all facing different sides of the competition space.

"Mallory's waving at us." Mom pulled on Brayden's arm, leading them to an empty station beside Ava and her mom. The whining he was certain he heard in her voice moments ago had given way to something bordering excitement.

"Oh, good, you two made it! We were starting to worry." Mallory handed over two aprons, but Brayden hardly realized it until she shoved it at his chest. He was too enamored with Ava and how adorable she looked in a snowman apron with her hair pinned up. He'd always found his duplex neighbor attractive, but something was different now. He couldn't put his finger on it, but whatever it was might have something to do with why his pulse tripled at the very sight of her cute smile.

"Hey," he said, like a shy teenaged boy who was lucky enough to secure one date with the prettiest girl in school. Brayden hadn't felt this way in years. It didn't matter what major life decisions waited for him or what might break them apart. He was falling for Ava, that much was clear.

"We weren't sure you were going to make it," Ava said, tucking a loose strand behind her ear, drawing his gaze to her exposed neck. Was he imagining the light flush of her cheeks, or simply taking credit for it? He yearned to nuzzle that soft spot with his lips. Would she giggle at the graze of his beard or complain that it was too scratchy?

"Mom got into the fudge."

Ava's face lit up. "She likes the basket?"

"I almost got her to admit it." They laughed together, reminding Brayden of the early days when he'd bought Mom gifts she scoffed at. They used to joke about it when Brayden stopped at the store and picked up yet another item. It wasn't the quality of the gifts, only that they'd come from the very place Brayden moved away to.

"C'mon, you two lovebirds," Mallory said, tugging on his arm. "Time for the briefing."

Brayden tried, oh how he tried, to listen to the rules, the time, the way the cookies would be judged. But he kept stealing glances at Ava, feeling a small victory every time she flashed him her shy smile. Something was definitely changing between them. He could turn down the CEO position. He'd have to come clean about his extra efforts to help save Ava's store and hope she understood why he kept it from her.

Brayden didn't want secrets between them anymore. Once the store was officially saved from foreclosure and that weight was off Ava's back, he'd confess it all, including how he didn't want their relationship to be fake, but real.

"Contestants, to your stations!" the mayor, Lee Daniels, announced. "We'll start in five minutes."

"Isn't this fun?" Mallory cooed, her arm latched around Mom's. Oddly enough, Brayden's mom only looked mildly uncomfortable, and he hadn't caught her once checking her phone while they were in the building. "I don't care which one of us wins," she added to the group, her voice dropped low. "So long as one of our teams beats Tillie Grant."

Ava laughed. "What do you have against her anyway?"

"Nothing," Mallory answered, though Ava suspected she wasn't being honest. "She's the one to beat. One of us beats her, we win the whole shindig."

"She has a kid as her teammate," Brayden added.

"That *kid* is Sophie's daughter, Caroline," Mallory explained. "Practically an understudy for Tessa Whitmore, well, Davies now. But you know what I mean. That girl's learned most of what she knows from a professional chef. Don't underestimate our competition."

At the chime of the timer, contestants instantly got to work. Glancing around the room, Brayden recognized nearly everyone competing, even if he couldn't place names to all of them. This place was special. "You remember when we used to make these?" Brayden asked, following Grandma's recipe to a tee. "Should've bought the sticks of butter sooner so they could soften."

"We improvise," Mom said clamping the foil-wrapped sticks in her hands. "Keep going. These'll be softer in a few minutes."

They worked in silence, like a well-oiled machine. They had the same business relationship as well, and he wondered if that was why Mom had never considered Sarra taking over the company. Mom and his sister often butted heads because they operated differently. Sarra was much more like their dad, bold and unafraid to speak her mind, even if her opinion was unpopular. "You used to love Christmas," Brayden said.

"I still love Christmas."

Brayden pinned her with a questionable stare. "You're more of a Scrooge than Ebenezer himself."

"Am not!"

"Do you remember when Christmas took over the entire house the weekend after Thanksgiving? When everyone else was out Black Friday shopping, we pulled out all the decorations from the attic."

Mom smiled fondly as she added the vanilla. "We had so much tinsel garland that you and your sister used to pretend to swim in it." Her smile faded.

"I didn't realize how much we stopped doing after your dad . . ."

Brayden squeezed Mom in a side hug. "I'm glad you're here for Christmas this year."

"Me, too."

As Brayden rolled out the dough, Mom turned his sloppy circles into perfect ones, adding garnishment for the Santa effect. Maybe they wouldn't win, but Brayden already felt he was strides ahead when it came to his relationship with his mom.

"Better make two sheets, just in case," Mom said, breaking off a piece of dough and slipping it to him. Just like old days.

"Good plan."

As Mom slipped the first pan into the oven, Brayden met Ava's glowing gaze. It warmed him from the inside out, making it harder to deny his growing feelings. Maybe he didn't *want* to deny them any longer.

"I like her, you know," Mom said as the mayor strolled from station to station, reporting the progress of each pair of contestants to the audience. "She's independent. Smart. She doesn't put up with any of your slack, but she cares a great deal about you. I recognize that look. I wore it often enough years ago." Mom swiped at her cheek with the side of her hand. "Flour, I think."

"I'm not ready to go back," Brayden said gently. "I have so much here."

"Mallory's done quite the job of showing me that," Mom admitted, perfecting the circles of cookie dough on their second pan. "Brayden, I have a confession."

He swallowed, uncertain whether he'd like what she had to say. With the mayor two stations away, he waited.

"I was only going to retire now because I wanted you to move home."

"What?"

Mom turned and looked him in the eyes. It was then he saw the glistening tears threatening to escape. "You're my son, Brayden, and I almost lost you. You're not the only one the accident rattled. Letting you drive all the way to Alaska, in the winter no less, after almost losing you was the hardest thing I've ever done."

Ignoring the mayor and the timer, Brayden pulled Mom into a tight hug. "I never knew you felt that way."

"I've gone two decades without being driven by

emotion," she said with a weak laugh. "Why would I start now?"

The mayor interrupted the moment, asking them a few questions about the recipe and how they expected the cookies to turn out. It was then, as he answered questions, that Brayden noticed the crowd gathering in the center. Hardly a seat remained empty.

"Good luck to you both!" Lee said with a nod, moving on to Ava's station.

Brayden pulled the first batch from the oven and slipped in the second pan. "I don't think I want to move back to Texas, Mom. Not now. Not in two years."

Mom nodded, but wouldn't meet his eyes. "I know. But I'd be lying if I said it didn't break my heart. Your father always envisioned the company staying in the family. When you were born, he used to talk about how proud he'd be to watch you run something he built from the ground up."

Guilt twisted inside him, but not enough to change his mind. "I think I might love her, Mom."

Mom patted his arm. "Maybe you should tell her. Your grandma was right. Time goes by faster than you think, and you never know when yours is up. If you don't want to run the company, I'll stay on a couple more years. Figure something out." She shoved at his arm. "Go tell her how you feel."

"Here?"

"They just put their cookies in the oven."

Brayden's heart thundered in his ears. It was time for this fake relationship to turn into a real one. "Okay."

Chapter Thirteen

Ava

"Can I talk to you for a second?" Brayden asked. From the corner of her eye, Ava'd watched him move from his station to their counter, her heart beating a little quicker with each step of his approach. Ava could hardly explain why this moment was any different than the hundreds of others they'd shared.

"Sure. What's up?"

Mom, knowing smile on her lips, nodded. "I need to chat with Pam for a moment. Mind that timer, Ava dear. We can't win with burned cookies, you know." She patted Ava on the arm, abandoning their station to give Ava some rare privacy.

Admittedly, Ava'd snuck a few too many glances at Brayden during the competition, something many audience members no doubt caught from their seats. It warmed her heart to see him getting along so well with his mom, but that wasn't why she was stealing peeks.

She liked him. *Really* liked him.

There was no point in lying to herself about it anymore. If she wasn't mistaken, he liked her, too. The whole running a company in Texas thing added a slight snafu. She couldn't sell the Forget Me Not and leave her hometown. She wouldn't. But maybe they could figure something out. Some sort of compromise where they could try out a *real* relationship. *Maybe he'll stay.*

For the first time in a while, she felt . . . hope.

"We should've teamed them up together," Brayden said with a nervous laugh, nodding at their mothers. "They seem to have become unexpected best friends."

"They have, haven't they?" Ava wiped her hands on a towel, though they weren't wet. "It's nice to see you and your mom getting along. Seems you two worked through some things." Yes, she was fishing. No, she didn't care.

"We did." Brayden's answer trailed off with his

vacant stare, but Ava couldn't even be upset about his vague answer. She was much too distracted by his presence.

"What did you want to talk to me about?" Ava asked, feeling like a nervous teenager hoping her crush might ask her to the prom. She welcomed the feeling over fear and anxiety about the store, even if it was only a brief distraction. "Brayden?"

"I, uh, wanted to tell you good luck. You and your mom." He nodded at the cookie sheet on the counter. "With the cookies."

Ava raised a challenging eyebrow. "That's it?"

"Maybe not."

"What's with you?" Ava teased. "You never get panicky or nervous, ever. Do you have something serious to tell me?"

"You might say that."

A glance at the oven timer warned they had less than five minutes before cookies needed to come out. "We can talk after—" Words froze when Ava's gaze fell past Brayden and landed on Laurel Evans. The two hadn't seen each other in years. How many, Ava was no longer sure. She'd lost count. A lifetime wouldn't be long enough. "You've got to be kidding me."

Brayden spun around, following her gaze. "Who's she?"

"She has some nerve." Ava's fists balled at her sides, watching Laurel laugh alongside one of her sisters, oblivious to the daggers Ava was shooting at her with her eyes. Worse, Kinley sat beside her. It was her best friend who first noticed Ava's narrowed glare. Apology flashed in her expression.

Ava pulled off her apron and threw it against the counter.

"Ava," Brayden said, his tone low and cautious as one set of eyes after another seemed to settle on her from the audience. "Don't do anything rash."

"Rash?" Ava repeated. That was exactly what she needed to do, something rash. Something drastic. Something that sent a clear message. But as a local business owner, she had a reputation to protect. She spun on her heel and marched to a side door without a coat to keep from causing a scene she couldn't take back. Her anger boiled hot enough to keep her plenty warm.

She made it across the street before Laurel called after her. "Ava, wait."

"Go. Away."

"Can we please talk?"

Ava continued marching toward her car, but

then remembered Mom had driven. Dang her luck. She headed for the intersection. A right turn would lead to her shop, three blocks away. She could run if it came down to it. She had time before frostbite was a serious concern.

"Ava, please." The crunch of snow behind her warned Ava that Laurel was running.

Ava picked up her pace, hoping to make the corner and take cover in the hardware store. She'd hide out in the storeroom if she had to. Harold wouldn't mind. At least, she hoped not. Black Bear Coffee was too far away unless she made a mad dash, and Laurel would follow her in anyway.

But at the corner, Ava came to an instant halt.

Ed stood on the sidewalk, munching on a wreath hanging from a light post. "You again?" Ava felt like screaming, but she kept her anger in check because a couple across the street was snapping pictures of the moose in downtown Sunset Ridge.

"Ava—"

Ava yanked Laurel hard by the arm to keep her from running out in front of her and startling Ed. In his current position, the giant moose was impossible to spot until one reached the corner of the brick bank building. She might have a grudge against her former best friend, but she didn't want her to get trampled by a berry-obsessed moose.

"Oh, my. I— Just wow." Laurel shuffled backward, her wide blue eyes never leaving Ed. "I forgot how *big* moose are."

"Guess they don't have a whole lot of those in the Bahamas or Cancun or wherever you've been."

"Florida," Laurel said.

"Oh, that's right." Ava spotted Kinley and Brayden, both trotting toward them with coats, and decided it was best to get her jabs in now before someone tried to silence her. "You save the extra exotic beach locations for secret elopements. Tell me, have you married anyone else since my brother? Or should I say how many?"

"Ava, that's not fair."

"Does Chase know you're back for a visit?"

"I'm not visiting."

Ava stared at Laurel as though she'd grown a second head. "What do you mean?"

"I moved back home." Because Ava was too stunned to warn Kinley and Brayden of the impending doom around the corner, Laurel did it for her. Ed huffed at the intrusion, but it wasn't enough for him to charge or abandon his post.

Seconds later, Brayden draped a coat over her shoulders and pulled her against him. She wanted to kick and scream. It was the least she should be allowed to do with everything on her plate. The store wasn't saved. Mom was still in town, all up in her business. Then there was the matter of her feelings for Brayden. Ava couldn't handle one more thing on her plate.

The last thing she could handle was Laurel. *Not now.*

"You're freezing," Brayden said, rubbing her arms. His magical ability to calm her didn't appear to be working. *Just my luck.* "We should get you back inside." Ava wanted to look into those reassuring eyes, but too many emotions coursed through her veins to trust a single one of them, no matter how tempting.

"I'm sorry," Laurel said.

"You're a few years too late," Ava muttered.

"I want to fix this," Laurel went on. "Ava, please. I'm sorry. I never meant to hurt you over this. I won't make excuses about past choices. I can't change anything."

"You're right, you can't."

Ed lifted his head at her sharp tone, his ears dropping then standing. The moose really did seem to have it out for her. Hadn't the universe given her enough obstacles for one season? She didn't need the town's favorite moose as her enemy too. She stared into those dark, wild eyes, realizing she'd rather befriend Ed than rip open old wounds with Laurel.

"We should get everyone back inside," Brayden said, urging Ava forward with his arm as Ed shuffled in place. It might mean nothing. Or it might mean he was tired of the snack-crashers and preparing a charge. "Ed, try across the street," he added to the moose over his shoulder when they were a safer distance away. "You might have better luck. Seems you picked this side pretty clean."

"Are those even real berries?" Kinley asked.

"Ed will tear apart every wreath in town until he finds some that are."

"Ava—"

"No, Kinley. You've picked your side."

"There aren't sides," Laurel practically shouted. "Ava, I want to help."

Ava turned sharply at that, her eyes narrowing at Laurel. "Help with *what*?"

"Don't pretend everything's fine. I know it's not."

Anger was easy enough to blame for her quickening pulse, but Ava couldn't deny the sliver of fear. The only person who knew about the financial situation of the Forget Me Not was Brayden. She looked up at him now, appreciating his willingness to stand by her even in her hardest, craziest moments. She felt embarrassed to be hashing this out in front of him. If he had been about to confess real feelings for her, he'd think twice about it now. Ava was stressed to her limit, and this was the cherry on the crappiest cake she'd ever been served. "You should leave while you still can," she said to him softly, apology in eyes. "This isn't what you signed up for. I wouldn't hold it against you."

"I'll go inside so you three can talk, but I'm not abandoning ship," Brayden said as they neared the door. "We can talk tomorrow. After we're done with the wedding." He squeezed her hand before he slipped inside.

She waited two beats after the door closed to face Kinley and Laurel. "You two happy, ganging up on me like this?"

"Ava, we just want to help," Kinley pleaded.

"I don't know what you're talking about."

"Oh, come on," Laurel said. "It's not that hard to figure out. You've been stressed out for weeks, from what Kinley's told me. Hiding some secret you won't share. Now you're making a thousand Christmas baskets last minute? We put the pieces together."

"It's not a thousand."

"Ava, we know something's going on," Kinley added, her tone much gentler. "Please, let us help. We're your best friends."

"No, you *were* my best friends." Tears stung the corners of her eyes. Ava wasn't ready to return to Town Hall, but standing out in the wintery air was out of the question. She was surprised Mom hadn't burst onto the scene. Luckily *someone* had to watch the cookies.

"Go ahead and be mad, but we're not giving up on you," Laurel said, stepping closer. Unless Ava wanted to be backed up against a frosted door, she had nowhere to go. "Whether you like it or not, you won't get rid of us so easily. We know the store's in trouble. We also know you don't like accepting help from anyone. It was the same when we were twelve, and it's the same now. You can be mad at me all you want, but I'm not turning my back on you now."

"You can call the cops on us for loitering at your store if comes down to it, but I wouldn't count on it doing much good," Kinley added, and the three finally cracked the faintest of smiles. "We won't say anything to your mom. Promise. But let us help."

"I don't need your help." But the declaration wasn't as firm as it was before. Ava was almost out of time, and despite how decent basket sales had been, they weren't enough. She'd only earned half the balloon payment. The clock was counting down at an alarming rate. "But *if* I did, what could you even do?"

"We have a few ideas," Kinley answered, a mischievous twinkle in her eyes. "Will you trust us?"

Ava shook her head, her anger dissolving with each passing second. She and Laurel could hash the past out later. Right now, she had to admit it felt pretty darn good to have her best friends in her corner, even if they'd muscled their way into it. "If I fail now, I only have myself to blame."

"And you'll know you turned down help that could've kept the doors open," Laurel shot back. "I've learned a thing or two while I was away. Give us a chance to show up for you, the way you've always shown up for us, even when we didn't deserve it."

"If I have to throw in your favorite blueberry scones to convince you, I will," Kinley added.

"Okay, fine. You can help. But not a word to anyone. Especially my mom. Brayden's the only one who knows, and he only found out by accident." With the words out, Ava felt instantly lighter. Maybe this was the Christmas miracle she didn't know she needed. She peered down the block, catching a quick glimpse of Ed as he crossed the street. "Sometimes I think that moose knows more than he lets on," she mumbled.

"What's that?" Laurel asked.

"Never mind." Ava spun back toward the door. "Let's get back to the competition before I get my mom disqualified. I'll never hear the end of it if that happens."

Chapter Fourteen

BRAYDEN

"I had no idea how they were going to pull off a winter wedding at the lodge," Ava said as Brayden helped her into her coat when they left Cadence and Ford's wedding reception. Faint music followed them down the hall, even with the doors closed behind them. "I have to admit, I'm impressed with how they utilized the lobby and that party room. They're bigger than they looked."

He held out his arm for Ava, knowing full well she had no reason to take it. The moms were downtown playing holiday bingo, something he never imagined he'd catch his mom doing in his lifetime.

Sunset Ridge had been better for her than he ever expected. He only wished he'd invited her sooner.

He and Ava had no one to pretend for, but she looped her arm through his anyway.

Because he'd made an early morning basket delivery to his contact in Anchorage so Ava could stay and handle the store, they hadn't had much time to talk since the blowout with her friends at the baking contest. But whatever had come of it, Ava appeared calmer today. Despite the looming deadline that was less than twenty-four hours away.

"Tomorrow's a big day, Christmas Eve and all," Brayden said as they neared the front door of the lodge, "but would you be willing to stay out a little while longer? I heard the northern lights are supposed to be absolutely brilliant tonight. We should go enjoy them."

Ava hesitated, as expected.

"You don't have a single basket left you *can* put together. You're not going to go peddle them tonight either. There's not a thing to do until morning where your shop is concerned. Give yourself a short break, Ava. Whatever fate befalls it, you've earned an hour off."

"I thought that's what the wedding was for," she teased.

"I meant some time for yourself." Brayden held the truck door open and waited until she was seated to close it. He hurried around the front, thankful for auto start, and jumped in. "Just an hour. Then if you want to go home, I'll take you straight there. I'll even bring you coffee in the morning."

"What about Elsie?"

"She had quite the day with a questionable tree branch after your mom slipped her that sugar cookie. I promise she won't mind my absence a little while longer. She's pretty wiped." Brayden knew Ava was out of objections and turned onto the back road through town that would lead them into total darkness within two miles.

Tonight, he planned to lay it all on the line. How he felt *and* the secrets he'd kept from her. Because tomorrow, if she couldn't sell enough baskets to save the store, he was writing her a check for the remaining balance. She could be mad at him all she wanted, but he wasn't going to let the Forget Me Not go out of business. Not tomorrow. Not ten or twenty years from now. He was in it for the long haul.

"You asked me something a few days ago," he said. "Something I didn't answer."

Ava let out a laugh. "*You* not answer a question? That never happens."

He yearned to take her hand, but the dark sky, so much blacker here in the winter than he'd ever seen anywhere else, demanded his full attention on the road. Ed could be around any turn. "You asked me why I moved to Sunset Ridge."

"Well?"

Brayden slowed for a curve, light snow flurries forming. He hoped clouds wouldn't cover the magnificent show. Not tonight. "I almost died."

"I don't understand."

Slowly, he took the turn to the lookout point, wanting to park before he continued. There were as many steep drop-offs here as where he'd been driving that day. Once he found the perfect spot, he shifted into park, unbuckled his seat belt, and turned. The dashboard lights illuminated the concern on Ava's pale face.

"When I lost my grandpa, I thought the best way to deal with that was to throw myself into work. Every waking second."

Ava turned in her seat, reaching over and placing her hand on top of his.

"I was on a conference call, driving through a particularly rocky area. I had the call on speaker," he added, knowing that didn't really make it any better. "But I was so preoccupied with winning over a new

207

client that I slipped off the side of the road. Soft shoulder after a heavy rain." Brayden paused as memories assaulted him, as clear now as they were that day. A byproduct of finally describing the tragedy out loud to another. He forced himself to push forward. "My truck tumbled down a rocky ledge and landed upside down in a creek that's normally pretty full. But we had a drought come through— Long story short, I should've died for so many reasons, but I walked away from that accident with hardly a scratch to show for it."

Ava squeezed his hand so hard he thought he might temporarily lose circulation. "That's awful that you had to go through that. I'm so grateful you survived. I—"

At the sight of a tear, Brayden reached out and brushed it away with his thumb. "That experience gave me pause. It caused me to take a step back and realize the path I was on wasn't the one I was destined to travel. My grandma begged me to take some time off, so I did."

"Then how did you end up *here*? From Texas."

His hand fell gently on her folded knee. "My grandparents honeymooned in Sunset Ridge. My grandma suggested it when I told her I was taking time off and getting away."

"So you just drove your truck to *Alaska* and ended up staying?"

Brayden shrugged. "Yeah, that's pretty much how it happened. I kept finding reasons to stick around and fewer reasons to go back. I was high up on the corporate ladder, but I found more purpose here."

"So your mom—"

"Will be fine. She didn't understand why I wanted to stay until she saw everything for herself. I half suspect she'll buy a vacation rental so she has an excuse to visit."

Ava's eyes illuminated. "You're staying?"

"I couldn't stand the thought of leaving."

"But your mom's company—"

"Will be fine without me." He wanted to kiss her again, but as he started to lean in, the first brush of color danced across the clearing sky. "The northern lights are out." He cut the headlights and pushed open his door. "Come on."

They met at the front of the truck, their gazes turned high up into the night sky. Brayden pulled Ava into his arms, her back against his chest, and they watched with rapt interest. Fluid strokes of green appeared, one by one, as if someone were running a paintbrush through the sky. With each

209

stroke, the lights danced and reshaped. Hints of purple came next.

"I've seen these lights so many times," Ava said as snow flurries lightly dusted her hat, "but it always feels extra special when they turn purple. A rare treat."

This. This moment was what he wanted. Maybe for the rest of his life.

The realization should've shocked Brayden. Maybe overwhelmed him with the urge to run. But instead, it calmed him. He had no doubts that Ava Monroe was his future. He'd stay in Sunset Ridge without her by his side, but his life was more colorful, like the skies above, with her a part of it.

"I don't want to do this fake relationship thing anymore," Brayden said.

Ava stiffened against him. "I shouldn't be surprised after yesterday—"

"That's not what I meant." He wriggled her out of his arms so he could spin her around to face him. Brayden cupped her cheek, tilting her head up until she met his gaze. "I don't want it to be *fake* anymore. I want to try this for real."

Ava's parted lips attempted to pass words, but the heavy emotion in her eyes said it all. "I'd like that."

With the northern lights above putting on quite the show, snow flurries dusting their coats and teasing the edges of Ava's hair, Brayden leaned in slowly, carefully. This wasn't to be a kiss forced under the mistletoe. As his lips gently brushed hers, he surrendered all his inhibitions to the moment. A moment he would cherish for the rest of his life.

Her arms wrapped around his neck, pulling him down as the kiss deepened.

Brayden could lose himself forever in this magical moment. He wanted to. But he had another confession to make. "I have to tell you something else," he said when their lips broke apart.

"No," Ava said with a shake of the head. "Not tonight."

"It's important," he implored.

"This is the first really wonderful moment I've had in a very long time." Her eyes sparkled and pleaded with his. Ava's hand combed through his beard, pulling him down to her eager and waiting lips, still slightly swollen from their last kiss. "Please, whatever it is, save it for tomorrow and kiss me again instead." He could no more deny her another than stop the clock from ticking forward.

Chapter Fifteen

Ava

"Coffee, as promised," Brayden said the next morning, handing Ava a cup after she locked her front door.

"Thank you." But her smile had much less to do with gratitude and a whole lot more to do with memories of their snowy kisses beneath the northern lights. She yearned to kiss him again, and almost did, except Laurel honked the horn. "Guess we better go. Big day and all."

The familiar knot in the pit of her stomach returned, reminding her how much was riding on today. Either she'd write a check that wouldn't bounce by the close of business, or the bank would assume ownership of the family store.

"Hey," Brayden said from the bottom step, blocking her escape, "It's going to be okay. I promise, that store will still be yours when the day is over. Whatever it takes."

Tempted to ask what that meant, Ava lingered on the stairs. "What did you want to tell me?" she asked instead. "Last night?"

Brayden traced his fingers down her cheek. A tactic no doubt meant to distract her, judging by the dimness he hid behind a smile. "We'll talk when the day is over."

"We need to go," Kinley called out the passenger window of Laurel's car. "Time's ticking."

Ava's best friends hadn't given her any clue what their plan might be. For all Ava knew, they were going to stand on the street corners with signs to spin or hold a parade. It didn't matter *what* their bright idea was, though. All that mattered was that Ava wasn't alone in this critical hour.

"I'll grab Elsie and meet you all at the store," Brayden said to Ava, kissing her gently on the lips. For a moment, every worry disappeared. "Merry Christmas Eve."

Ava hurried into the back seat of Laurel's SUV,

her lips still buzzing and fingers tingling. How one simple brush of their lips could make her dizzy was a mystery Ava didn't care to solve.

"You two sure have gotten cozy," Kinley said. "He does know that we know the truth, right? You two don't have to pretend in front of us."

Ava bit down on her bottom lip, but her enormous smile won out in the end. "It's not fake anymore."

At a stop sign, both Laurel and Kinley turned their heads and stared at Ava. "What?"

Giddiness filled Ava, and she found she rather preferred this feeling over the anxiety and gloom of these past several months. "We decided to try it for real."

"That's great!" Kinley squealed. "I'm so happy for you!"

"How much do you know about this Brayden character?" Laurel asked, her voice much too serious for so happy a moment.

Kinley whapped Laurel with the back of her hand. "You could've waited until *after* Christmas," she muttered.

This dynamic certainly reminded her of the old days. "Out with it," Ava ordered. "If you know something, you better spit it out right now."

"I did some research on him," Laurel said, her eyes locked on the road in front of her. "Seems no one in town knows who he really is, so it made me curious. Did you know he's a multi-millionaire?"

"What?" Ava was certain Laurel made a mistake. "His *mom* has all the money," she countered. "He's just a regular guy. I'd know if Brayden was secretly wealthy." *Or would I?*

"He's worth eight figures, Ava," Kinley said. "There was an article in a business magazine a couple of years back. So, unless he gave away his fortune—"

"Which he didn't, because he's bought up a bunch of properties in town. Under the company Northern Lights Property," Laurel added.

"He owns that?" Ava asked, her words barely above a whisper. "He's *my* landlord?" Ava was taken aback by the news. She tried not to let it upset her. People were entitled to their anonymity, after all. Though it made a lot more sense now why her December rent had been waived. And the gift basket from her landlord . . . "So what if he has money and doesn't want people to know? I think it speaks more about his character that he doesn't flaunt his wealth. Don't you?"

Laurel turned onto the main strip and headed up

the hill toward the Forget Me Not. "He's in line to take over one of the most successful marketing firms in the country. He's the reason that company has grown at the rate it has. He's about as far from an Average Joe as they come."

Ava let out an annoyed sigh. "Are you trying to ruin my happiness or something?" Ava shot at Laurel. "I know this already. He's not going back. He told me last night. Unless you know something that actually matters, drop it."

"It's just that I don't get why he doesn't make a donation or something to the store," Laurel continued. "Kinley told me about that massive order you received. The one from a company in Anchorage."

"What about it?" Ava asked through gritted teeth.

"We may have peeked at your notes last night when you were at the wedding. That company is one of the major clients he won for Young Elite Marketing Services two years ago. I made a call and found out he worked with that Vanessa Stinson specifically on that account. I thought her showing up and ordering seventy-five baskets was . . . strange." Laurel pulled into a parking spot, and it was then that Ava noticed how full the parking lot already was. "Did you know your best customer is his grandma?"

Ava's head was spinning, and she didn't like it one bit. She recalled all the decorations throughout his house, ones from *her* store. Had Brayden been secretly trying to save the store and letting her believe she was doing it on her own? "Stop," she pleaded. "Please, just stop." She pushed out of the SUV, but before she could make it to the front door, Brayden stood in her path.

"Hey, Elsie's in the truck—"

"You *lied* to me."

"I—"

"How many things have you done in secret?" She practically growled the words at him, but it was that or yell and cause a scene. "And why did I have to hear about it from my *friends*?"

"Ava—"

"Go. Just go. I'm done doing this." She pushed him out of the way and marched straight for the door. She couldn't abandon her store today of all days, but she needed to hide out in her office for a few minutes. Just long enough to drink her coffee and keep from hyperventilating. Then she'd face her customers with a smile, even if it killed her.

But she hardly had the door closed before she

screamed. "Mom, what are you doing in here? It was locked. Do you still have a key?"

"Ava dear, you never told me." Her tone was eerily quiet, forlorn. She held a ledger book up in explanation. One with the final notice letter wedged in as a bookmark. *Well, jingle bells.*

Ava groaned. "I knew I should've switched completely to electronic." She pulled out her chair, fell into the seat, and dropped her head onto the desk. Coffee couldn't fix this day. Nothing could.

"Why didn't you tell me you took out a second mortgage?" Mom asked gently, as if hurt to be left out of such a big secret. "I would've loaned you the money myself."

"I wanted to prove to you I could do this on my own," Ava said without lifting her head. "You retired *four* years ago, but you still criticize every decision I make." She forced herself to sit up and face Mom's hurt gaze. "I wanted to prove I could do this without needing my hand held. If you loaned me the money, you would've been calling all the shots."

"That's not true."

Ava stared at her mom, an eyebrow raised in challenge.

"Okay, fair point." Mom sat on the edge of the

desk, but when it wobbled, she stood up. "Can't believe you kept this old thing."

"Not by choice." Ava shook her head, popping out of her chair to pace the cramped room. "Mom, I love you. But you have to let the store go. Whether it's successful or I run it into the ground—which we'll know in a few hours—I need to do it on my own."

"You always were so stubbornly independent," Mom mumbled. "Ava, you don't have to do anything alone. That's the beauty of a small community. Even your Brayden has figured that out, and he's as city as they come." Mom moved around the desk and trapped Ava with hands on her arms. "Listen." She nodded toward the door. "You hear that? That's a *full* store. That's your friends, your family, your community showing up in your time of need."

"But—"

"Your Christmas baskets were brilliant, by the way. You and I both know they would've sold better earlier in the season, but I'm not criticizing you for it. It's something to remember for next year."

"What's your point?"

"I made more mistakes than you can begin to imagine. I had your dad to fall back on, though. There's nothing wrong with accepting help, Ava dear. I never would've had a store to hand down if I tried to do it all myself."

Ava felt the knot in her stomach tighten. "I've made a mess of things."

"Look at me," Mom ordered. "You're going to drink that coffee, fasten that smile, and get out there. We're going to save the Forget Me Not Boutique today, and you're going to let everyone who wants to help, help." She patted Ava hard on the arm. "And Brayden, that man adores you. He told me everything he's done to help you, despite the wrath he's feared all along. You should feel so lucky to have such a man in your corner."

"Well, now I feel even worse," Ava groaned.

"First, we save the store. Then, you make amends with Brayden." Mom squeezed her in a suffocating hug. "It'll all work out, sweetie. I promise it will."

Chapter Sixteen

BRAYDEN

"You're hiding out here on Christmas Eve?" Mom's voice pulled him from his most important project, but only briefly. The desk had to be perfect, and he still wasn't satisfied with the details. It might not be enough to repair the damage between them, but he wanted Ava to have it anyway.

"There's coffee brewing," he said, a slight smile forming as Mom greeted Elsie with a few pats. He would be sad to see her go. "You still headed out on a flight tomorrow morning?"

"Afraid so," she answered, ignoring the coffee and taking a seat on the cot nearby. She set a covered plate of food on an end table, reminding him how long it'd been since he ate. He'd been invited to Chase's place for Christmas Eve dinner, but had opted out to give Ava space. "What happened with you and Ava?"

Brayden shouldn't be surprised at the question. He'd done as Ava asked today and steered clear of her. But he hadn't stopped helping. He printed more flyers and spread them all over town. Stopped people in the streets and encouraged them to check out the last-minute gift ideas. He also snuck some hundred-dollar bills in the donation jar—Kinley and Laurel's brilliant idea—before he dipped out of sight.

"Secrets," Brayden muttered in response. "Too many secrets."

"I thought you cleared all that up."

"Tried to, but her friends beat me to it."

"You could always come back to Texas."

Brayden stared hard at his mom until a smile broke through her lips.

"I want you to be happy, Brayden. You'll sort things out with Ava, but be honest from here on out. No more secrets. She's not just some girl next door you're dating. You and I both know that." She forced him to stand and give her a hug. "I don't suppose I can convince you to take a break?"

"Sorry, I need to get this done."

"Well, if you change your mind." Mom nodded, heading to the door.

"Mom?"

She turned, her head cocked to the side and a slight smile on display.

"The company can still stay in the family without me or you running it. You should have a conversation with Sarra."

Mom nodded. "I'll do that."

Brayden turned back to the desk. It would mean working all through the night, but he was determined to get it finished in time for Christmas. Even if Ava didn't forgive him, she'd worked hard and persevered to save the store, and she deserved a proper desk from which to run her empire.

"Might as well settle in, Elsie," he said to the dog who was eyeing her bed. "It's going to be a long night."

Chapter Seventeen

Ava

Ava waited by her sliding glass door for over thirty minutes on Christmas morning, but Elsie didn't appear for her daily treat. If it weren't for the fresh tire tracks leading into Brayden's garage last night, undisturbed by snow or beast, she might've guessed he left town.

She wanted to be mad. Brayden hadn't kept one secret from her, but many.

She'd tossed and turned all night, upset with him for missing Christmas Eve dinner, but never once texting him to see where he was. It wasn't fair to expect him to show up when she told him to go away and he listened. Mostly, she was mad at herself.

It wasn't the secrets themselves that bothered her when she really got down to it. It was that he felt the need to keep them because of how she'd react to his help. Mom was right—not something she'd often admit—but Ava couldn't do this alone. Pride would be the end of the Forget Me Not Boutique before anything else. The store was saved for now. But hardship might visit her again in the future. She didn't want to face it alone.

Not anymore.

Staring out the back door, she caught a blur in the woodworking shop window. "What are the odds he was telling the truth back then?" she murmured, slipping on a pair of boots over her Christmas moose pajama bottoms.

Halfway to the shop, Ava spotted a moose in the tree line. "Ed," she mumbled with an amused shake of her head. "We don't have any more wreaths," she called to him. "You ate them all." She waited, expecting Ed to intervene. He was good at that. But he seemed to give her a head nod before he turned and tromped off into the neighborhood. "Merry Christmas to you, too," she murmured, a slight smile gracing her lips.

Ava scurried through the deep snow, attempting to follow Brayden's trail of footsteps. But snow crept into the top of her boots anyway. By the time she reached the shop, her calves were frigid.

"Brayden?" she called, shivering at the chill in the air. "Are you in here?"

Elsie trotted to her, tail wagging in greeting. Ava pulled a treat from her pocket and handed it over. "Merry Christmas, girl. This is just the stocking stuffer." She rubbed the golden behind the ears. "I have more presents for you under the tree."

"Ava?" Brayden looked half asleep from where he stood in the middle of the shop. The yawn solidified it.

"I should've brought coffee." She dared to step closer, the urge to be in his arms overwhelming. She didn't want to face another day without Brayden by her side. She realized last night how she truly felt, and she wanted very much to tell him. "You fell asleep out here?"

"Happens sometimes," he said with a mild shrug.

"You stayed out here all night?" She took a few steps closer. Had he been telling the truth all along? How could she have been so closed-minded and blithely shut him down all the times he tried to convince her? How much time had she wasted because of it? "On Christmas Eve?"

"Had something to finish." He stepped to the side, revealing a beautiful cherry desk. The fresh stain glistened in the sunlight, but it was the cubbies built up on the corners that drew her eyes. Slots for books, files, office supplies. This desk was an organizer's dream come true.

"Who's the lucky recipient?"

"You."

"Me?" Her heart swelled and happy tears stung her eyes. "You made this for me?"

"Of course I did." Brayden spun around, digging through a paper bag on a nearby end table. "And these too. Sorry they're not wrapped." He handed over a pair of plum-colored gloves, handmade in Ninilchik.

"You bought these at my store," she said with a laugh, swiping at a silly tear.

"It's the best place in town to shop." He took a step closer. One that eliminated the distance between them. "I'm surprised you still have your fingers after weeks of running around gloveless."

"Brayden, I'm sorry."

"Me, too." He cupped her arm with one hand, the heat of his touch warding off the chill of the shop.

"I shouldn't have kept all those secrets from you. I only meant to help, but now I see how wrong it was. I won't be keeping any more. Ask me anything you want, and I promise to work on my vagueness issue."

She let out a laugh. "I'm sorry you felt you had to keep any of it a secret from me. My stupid pride got in the way. I appreciate your help more than you know. My store would be closed for good if it wasn't for everything you did to help me."

Brayden looked up, and Ava followed his gaze.

"Mistletoe." Ava chuckled. "Hung that last night, did you?"

"Maybe." He dipped his head, capturing her lips with his own. Mistletoe kisses were quickly becoming her favorite. She might hang it everywhere next Christmas. "I did lie about one thing, or omitted anyway."

Ava pulled back enough to stare into his eyes. "What?"

"I don't only want a real relationship with you. I want a whole lot more. I love you, Ava Monroe. I think I've loved you for months." He kissed her again before she could respond, and she sank into the heart-fluttering sensation of his lips moving against hers. She could kiss him all day.

Elsie whined at the door.

"I better get a shower," Brayden said. "Your mom'll kill us if we miss Christmas morning."

"That she will." Ava pulled Brayden back by the arm. "I love you, too, you know. I'm really glad you're staying." She thought he might kiss her again, but Elsie started barking at the door.

"Better let her check out the questionable tree branch, or we'll never hear the end of it."

Despite the interruption, Ava's heart was full. So very full. She couldn't have asked for a better Christmas gift than everything she received this year.

Epilogue

CHASE

The only reason Chase Monroe attended his sister's New Year's Eve party was because his buddy Ryder strong-armed him into it. A guilt trip about bailing on him and leaving him alone to the women after Ryder helped him lay hardwood flooring. Never mind that Brayden was here, too. Ryder'd thrown in a free weekend for Chase to use his fishing boat, and that twisted his arm the rest of the way.

"You going to tell her?" Ryder asked, his voice low below the Christmas music. Didn't matter that Christmas was over. Ava would play holiday tunes as long as she could get away with it.

"I'll have to at some point," Chase answered in a mumble, his gaze drifting to his ex-wife for the tenth time since he arrived. *Wife. Not ex. Not technically.* Five long years and she still looked as stunning as the day he first kissed her.

"Not something you should keep from her," Ryder added seconds before his fiancée Kinley crashed their conversation in the corner and wrapped both hands around his arm. His serious expression morphed into a goofy, lovestruck grin in a heartbeat. "If you'll excuse me."

Ryder left him with a stern look—a not-so-gentle nudge.

Yes, Chase should tell Laurel they were still married. That some missed signature on the paperwork found earlier this year made the whole divorce null and void. Part of him wondered whether she already knew. Was that the reason she finally returned to Sunset Ridge? *No, it couldn't be.* Laurel would've hunted him down by now if that were the case.

Chase stalled a few minutes longer, watching his sister with Brayden as he sipped on his soda near the Christmas tree. No alcohol for the deputy fire chief. He had to be ready for a call should one come in.

He'd suspected from the day he ran into Ava and

Brayden outside Davies Hardware Store that their pretend relationship wouldn't remain fake too long. He was happy he was right; happy for Ava. He used to look at Laurel the way Brayden looked at Ava.

Now, with Laurel Evans having moved home, he wasn't sure how to feel besides twisted and torn. So much hurt lingered from their goodbye. Yet her smile, still radiant as the midnight sun, made him wonder if she'd healed. They would always mourn the loss, but maybe they could give things another go. She hadn't moved home with another man, after all. That had to mean something.

He was taking another sip when he spotted Laurel slip into the bathroom. He emptied his cup and snuck down the hallway to wait.

Chase had never stopping loving Laurel. What if the missing signature was fate's way of granting them a second chance?

"Laurel," Chase said, gently tugging at her elbow before she could hurry back to the festivities in the living room.

"Chase." Her expression went completely blank.

"Can we talk?"

"Now's not the best time. I should get back—"

"Please. It's important."

Laurel let out a heavy sigh, closing her eyes for

several beats. When she looked back up at him, any hint of the love they'd shared seemed gone. *Maybe it's just masked.* Laurel was a master at hiding her emotions. "I'm not home for you."

Chase took the gut punch with surprising grace. "I need to tell you something," he insisted. "It's important. It can't—"

Laurel held her hand up. "No."

At the slight strain in her voice, the urge to draw her into his arms overwhelmed him. "What's wrong?"

"Nothing."

He dared to touch her elbow again, unsurprised that the tingles from years ago returned. "You might fool everyone else, Laurel, but you never could lie to me."

She glanced down the hall, but no one came in search of either of them. "You can't tell anyone, Chase. I mean it."

"You know I keep a secret better than anyone." Their locked gazes spoke volumes. Despite how much pain he'd endured when they lost the baby and Laurel left town, making him swear never to tell anyone, he'd kept his promise. He kept it for her. "Tell me what's going on."

"It's Haylee." *Laurel's youngest sister.* A thousand possibilities zipped through his mind as he waited for her to explain. "She's . . . pregnant."

Chase blinked at Laurel, certain he'd heard her wrong. Haylee was the youngest of the Evans siblings. Too young to be having a baby of her own. She'd just left for college this past fall.

"It's a long story," Laurel said. "No one knows, not even my parents. I'm here for Haylee. She and her baby are all that matter right now. So whatever important thing you have to tell me, it has to wait until after her baby is born. I can't handle anything else right now." Such pain lingered in those soft blue eyes. "I just can't."

"I understand." It had to be stressful enough for her youngest sibling to be unexpectedly pregnant. He didn't have to ask about the father. Laurel wouldn't be here if the father were in the picture. But he was most concerned about Laurel's pain and how the loss of their own child would affect her now. "Are you okay?"

Tears glistened in her eyes. "I have to be."

"I'm here if you need anything, Laurel. I mean it."

"Thank you." She turned back toward the party, but Chase caught her wrist.

"I need to tell you—" Chase's radio chose that

moment to sound. *A call, now?* He looked at Laurel with regret, but she appeared relieved at the interruption. Relief wouldn't be too frequent a visitor for her these next several months. He had to let this go; hold on to it for later. They could sort everything out after her niece or nephew was brought safely in the world.

"You're good at keeping secrets," she said. "Keep yours a few months longer. I'm not going anywhere."

Sign up for Jacqueline Winter's newsletter to receive alerts about current projects and new releases!

http://eepurl.com/du18iz

Other Books by Jacqueline Winters

SWEET ROMANCE

Sunset Ridge Series

Starlight Cowboys Series

1 - Cowboys & Starlight

2 - Cowboys & Firelight

3 - Cowboys & Sunrises

4 - Cowboys & Moonlight

5 - Cowboys & Mistletoe

6 - Cowboys & Shooting Stars

Christmas in Snowy Falls

1 - Pawsitively in Love Again at Christmas

2 - Pawsitively Home for Christmas

3 - Pawsitively Yours for Christmas

Stand-Alone

*Hooked on You

STEAMY ROMANTIC SUSPENSE

Willow Creek Series

1 - Sweetly Scandalous

2 - Secretly Scandalous

3 - Simply Scandalous

About the Author

Jacqueline Winters has been writing since she was nine years old when she'd sneak stacks of paper from her grandma's closet and fill them with adventure. She grew up in small-town Nebraska and spent a decade living in beautiful Alaska. She writes sweet contemporary romance and contemporary romantic suspense.

She's a sucker for happily ever after's, has a sweet tooth that can be sated with cupcakes, and is a dog mom to a lovable Alaskan Husky. On a relaxing evening, you can find her at her computer writing her next novel with her faithful dog poking his adorable nose over her keyboard, demanding treats and/or pets. Usually both.